THE COMMANDERS' MATE

INTERSTELLAR BRIDES® PROGRAM - BOOK 15

GRACE GOODWIN

Published by KSA Publishers
Goodwin, Grace
The Commanders' Mate, Book 15
Cover design copyright 2019 by Grace Goodwin
Images/Photo Credit: Period Images; BigStock: forplayday

INTERSTELLAR BRIDES® PROGRAM

YOUR mate is out there. Take the test today and discover your perfect match. Are you ready for a sexy alien mate (or two)?

VOLUNTEER NOW!

interstellarbridesprogram.com

GET A FREE BOOK!

JOIN MY MAILING LIST TO BE THE
FIRST TO KNOW OF NEW RELEASES,
FREE BOOKS, SPECIAL PRICES AND
OTHER AUTHOR GIVEAWAYS.

http://freescifiromance.com

CHAPTER 1

Commander Karter, Battleship Varsten, Sector 438

"You shouldn't be here, Commander. I can take care of this." My second in command, Vice Commander Bard, walked next to me, shoulder to shoulder, as he had for over a decade. We were both battleship-born Prillon warriors, and I counted on him to speak the truth when I didn't want to hear it.

Bard spoke the truth now. Being in this wreck of a battleship was not the wisest course of action I could have taken. Yet, I had no choice. I had to see the level of destruction for myself. Commander Varsten was an excellent strategist, a seasoned warrior, and he was missing. I could not quite believe that half of his battle fleet had been destroyed in a matter of hours. Battlegroup Varsten had been decimated.

"The comm would not have done it justice." Some things needed to be witnessed.

Bard stepped over a pool of scorched blood on the floor, a frown on his usually blank face. "No, it would not."

When the comms came in from the survivors, I had not believed them, could not believe that nearly an entire battle-group had been wiped out so quickly.

Yet, here we stood in the scarred remains of a ship that had once housed nearly two thousand warriors, mates and children. Outside, three of Varsten's support vessels had been obliterated, not much more than fragments left spinning in the deep black of space. The battleship itself now drifted toward the nearest planet, weak engines not quite able to resist the relentless pull of gravity with the main power source destroyed. The metal corridors creaked and moaned beneath our boots as we pulled the foul scent of charred ship and death into our lungs through our helmets.

The devastation was vast. This section had a hull breach and our helmets, with supplemental oxygen, were required, as there was no air to breathe. Only half of the large vessel was still intact, and what was left was empty. A handful of dead were all that remained. Thank fuck we'd not come across a single murdered woman or innocent child in our search. It seemed the warriors who called this ship home had managed to get their families off the vessel but how that was even possible remained a mystery. Fuck, this entire situation had endless questions yet to be answered.

We walked the corridors of Commander Varsten's battle-ship. Not my ship. Not my people. Not my sector of space. But they were all mine now. The dead lining these corridors and floating in the cold emptiness of space just outside the ship were my people. This barely-functioning craft was now under my control.

They were mine. With their commander missing, the survivors who'd lived through the direct attack on this ship, as well as those in the battlegroup who'd been sent to safety, were my responsibility. And there were a shocking number of Varsten's people packed into the remaining cargo and support ships hiding on the other side of the nearest planet's star. It was as if Varsten had known the attack was coming and ordered all his people and half of his fleet out of danger right before the Hive could strike.

But that made no sense. Why would he evacuate non-essential personnel and knowingly move an elite class battleship into a trap? Why sacrifice a battleship and multiple support crafts? Leave Sector 438 open to Hive occupation? This area of space was neighbor to mine. Varsten and I had spoken often over comms, discussed strategy and Hive activity. He had been a patient male with two decades more battle experience than I. A wise commander. He wouldn't have done anything without reason. Finding out what had happened here was my first priority.

As was hunting and destroying the Hive attack fleet that had caused such destruction. I'd been transported here from Battleship Karter, along with an entire squadron of medical, military and support personnel, after receiving the distress call from those sent to safety. But they had not called during the Hive attack, but after it was over.

Hours after. We still had no explanation for that.

Seven hours, to be exact. We'd received a comm call from those who had been hiding on the other vessels. Unfortunately, there were no high-ranking officers among them. No one seemed to know what had pushed Commander Varsten to make such radical and inexplicable decisions.

Nothing made sense. Nothing.

"Where is the command crew?" I asked.

"We don't know." Our boots echoed with each stride as he answered me. "Those who are left of Varsten's battlegroup remain on the other side of the star. The star's radioactive field is interfering with our short-range comms and they are refusing to activate their quantum comm links."

"You're telling me he cleared his entire battlegroup of

3

GRACE GOODWIN

people, minus the command crew, into hiding, into... what, safety?"

He nodded. "It appears exactly that."

"Do we have ships in Sector 437 available to come here and escort them safely through a manual evacuation? The Coalition will not want to abandon these vessels." The other cargo and support vessels—the ones that had remained clear of the attack—had transport technology, but they were not equipped to handle the transport of nearly five thousand people.

The main battleship housed one-thousand four hundred warriors and family, as well as acted as the landing base for smaller assault ships. The ship itself was heavily armored and loaded with blaster technology in order to defend the smaller ships around it. Each commander of a battlegroup was in charge of one battleship and ten to twelve smaller support ships. Each group, referred to as a battlegroup, was named after their commander and responsible for one sector of space. Fully staffed, a complete battlegroup, all ships, held nearly five thousand people.

That were too many to transport in a short amount of time. Short-range attack ships from Battleship Karter would not be able to make it all the way to Sector 438 without assistance, and the ships still here in the dock of Battleship Varsten were all but destroyed.

The best option was to transport as many people as possible to Battlegroup Karter and send the remaining cargo and support vessels from Varsten's fleet on a direct course to intercept with the Karter and her ships as quickly as possible. But that would mean the smaller ships from Varsten's group would be unescorted and vulnerable to attack. And even that was assuming Prime Nial and the other fleet commanders would be willing to surrender this sector of space.

4

Not likely. Odds were Prime Nial would command me to split my fleet and resources and hang on to *both* Sector 437 and 438 until Commander Varsten's fleet and personnel could be replaced. Prime Nial would commission a new battleship and assign a new commander to this area. But that would take time.

Time the Hive might not give us.

Bard sounded as grim as I felt. "A few. If the survivors left now, they would rendezvous with our support ships in about thirty-six hours, but Varsten's pilots are refusing to move. They said they are under strict orders from Commander Varsten not to move yet, but they don't know why."

"And where the hell is Commander Varsten?" That was the question I most needed an answer to. Where was my old friend, and what the fuck had he been thinking?

Bard's lips pressed into a thin line. "Dead. They found his body in the pilot's seat of an attack shuttle. He was flying support, protecting the main ship. And he was alone."

"No co-pilot?" He was dead, and so, it seemed, were my hopes of getting some answers.

"No one. No navigation. No comms. He was running solo."

Another mystery I had no time to solve. Almost five thousand people were currently stranded on ships meant to sustain half that. And their battleship was gone. Well, we stood on what was left of it. Non-functioning and uninhabitable. Even if the rest of the Varsten's battlegroup moved out from behind the star, they would have no battleship to protect them. If they returned... if we left them here, alone and unprotected, they'd be ripe for Hive capture. That would mean five thousand new Hive drones, soldiers, breeders.

No.

"How many survivors on the other forward ships? Do we

have a body count?" I asked. Only a handful of dead warriors littered the corridors. I hated to think the Hive had taken the rest. It didn't seem possible, but then, I'd seen worse things.

Bard looked down at the tablet he carried. "Only three survivors so far. We've counted twenty dead, including Commander Varsten, but we haven't searched the entire ship."

"What the fuck was he thinking?"

Vice Commander Bard didn't respond to my question. I knew he didn't have that answer. Instead, he said, "Two members of his command crew have been transported to ReGen pods back on the Karter."

Gods be damned, maybe they would know what was going on here. "And the other survivor?"

When my second didn't speak immediately, I stopped walking, forcing him to do the same. He was a strong Prillon warrior, and I trusted his judgment and his instincts. In this instance, his silence sent alarms through my system. As if the annihilation of almost an entire battlegroup wasn't bad enough. Battlegroup Varsten had been protecting Sector 438 since I was a boy. The devastation around me was unthinkable. As was Varsten's death.

"He's I.C. and he's not talking."

I closed my eyes for a moment, let that extra level of insanity sink in. I.C. Intelligence Core. The dark side of the fleet. "Fuck. Where is he? I'll make him talk."

Bard arched a brow. "Should we get a message to Commander Phan?" He grinned, his copper skin and bronze eyes narrowing with anticipation. "I'm sure she would love to take a pound of flesh from one of her own."

A few years ago, that would have been true. Now, the Earthling was a mother. A mate. And permanently under my command. She had saved my entire battlegroup not long ago, she and the contaminated beast she'd shown up with dismantling a network of invisible mines the Hive had placed in space. Those mines had been trapping my entire group of ships. "She's too valuable. I won't risk bringing her here."

The hiss of burst vent pipes, the groan of metal as it shifted after the explosion, the deep command of voices in the distance delegating tasks to clean up this clusterfuck surrounded us. Destruction was nothing new to me, but this was... personal. Close to home, at least as close to a home one could have on a fucking battlegroup.

"You're here," he countered.

"I am nothing," I said simply.

Bard opened his mouth to argue, closed it. He knew how I felt about this. I was a warrior first and always. I fought. I killed. I protected my people, the people who became mine through Hive destruction. And if I died? So be it. Another member of my military family, or another worthy Prillon warrior, would take command. I was a cog in the wheel of the Coalition Fleet. I was a warrior. Nothing more.

"Chloe is I.C., Karter," he continued. "She can take care of herself." I often questioned the supposed *intelligence* of this group as they caused us more trouble than they were worth most of the time. But then, every once in a while, someone like Commander Chloe Phan came along and saved us all. I hated their secrets, but like all warriors, I recognized that spies and black-ops were a necessary evil. No battle commander could win a war without good intelligence on the enemy. And the hard-core bastards who served in the I.C. were the best. Including Commander Phan of Earth. But she was also mine to protect, a mate to two of my best warriors and a mother to their children. There was no need for her to risk herself out here in this chaos, especially when we had zero answers. I could beat the hell out of a tight-lipped I.C. commander all by myself.

"She's a mother," I said.

7

Bard grinned. "I'm going to tell her you said that."

"Why don't you tell Dara and her baby brother that you risked their mother's life for your entertainment?" It was my turn to smile, and I made sure to show every inch of my teeth —the better to rip Bard's throat out with. "If you make my Dara cry, I will destroy you."

We walked on.

Dara was beautiful, with black hair and green eyes, just like her mother. I loved her like she was my own. She was small, but fearless. And the moments she wrapped her small hand around mine were the only times I felt like more than a killing machine. I would do nothing to hurt her small heart, including risking her mother's life when it wasn't absolutely necessary. Her baby brother Christopher was full of fire and curiosity, a bright, daring child. But it was Dara's sweet innocence that kept me sane, gave me a reason to keep fighting.

Bard insulted me with laughter but kept further opinions to himself as he took me to the lone survivor on the command deck of the small cargo ship. We stepped over the dead as we went, a killing rage boiling hotter with each drop of blood that clung to my boots.

"Why did they leave the dead?" Bard asked.

Normally, a Hive attack resulted in a complete loss of all personnel. No bodies. No survivors. The Coalition Fleet had always assumed the Hive did something unpalatable with the dead, but I didn't ask the I.C. I had no desire to know the answer. What they did to the living was horror enough, and I struggled with my nightmares as it was. "I don't know. Maybe the I.C. officer will have answers for us."

Answers I didn't want. But *want* was a luxury I gave up years ago.

Within a few minutes, we rode the remaining functional lift to the command deck of the battleship and entered through an emergency airlock set up by my crew. Once inside, Bard and I removed our helmets and looked around. A Prillon warrior sat in the navigator's seat, head in his hands. His hair was golden and fair, as was his skin. He was large, his body a mountain in the small chair. But when he turned to face me, my body froze in shock.

CHAPTER 2

Erica Roberts, Interstellar Brides Processing Center, Earth

*E*verything was dark, but I could hear my warriors moving to surround me, touch me.

Claim me.

I'd been waiting for this for weeks, longing for them to give in and take me as one in front of the others...

That thought stopped me cold and my heart raced, the hard memory of the processing chair back in that cold, clinical room at the bride testing center intruded on my bliss, as did the pounding of my heart, not in fear, but in anticipation.

For as much as this woman's mind, whoever she was, wanted this claiming, I wanted it, too. This wasn't my body. In some far off, rational part of myself I knew that. But it felt real.

It was a dream. But it wasn't. But it sure as fuck *felt* real. It was real, to her, and somehow I was to share it with her.

When a large hand settled around my neck and my mate's warm chest pressed to my bare back, I slipped back into the dream, or hallucination—whatever this was. I didn't care if it was real or not. I *needed* my mates to touch me.

The warrior behind me tilted my chin up, warm hand around my throat a blatant mark of ownership. Around us I heard male voices chanting, at least six, perhaps seven, watching.

No, witnessing this claiming. My mates' honored chosen, sworn to protect me. They would watch...

Before my mind could follow that path, the male at my back slipped a finger into my aching pussy and I gasped, arching against him.

"So wet, mate. Are you ready for us?" His pleasure at my eagerness thrummed through our link, the mating collar I felt wrapped around my neck. Somehow it connected us. All three of us. How? I had no idea. I just felt.

My mind again surged forward, creating a haze of confusion as I processed the other woman's thoughts. Three of us? I had two mates? Did I want two mates? Two mouths. Four hands.

Two cocks.

And one of them had a finger in my pussy.

God, yes. It was all I could think about, melting into a puddle of need between two hard Prillon warriors. *My warriors.*

Which is how I knew that my primary male was watching us, his cock hard and heavy with need, holding himself back to prolong the pleasure of this moment. His emotions, his lust, were drowning me, overwhelming both of us through the collars as my second mate pumped his thick fingers in and out of my pussy. I wanted them to fuck me, claim me, make me theirs. Now. I was ready to surrender, give them everything, scream in pleasure in front of the whole damn ship if I had to.

I needed them. Inside me. I needed to come.

Need. Need. Need.

Anxious, I tried to reach for him but found my arms tied loosely above my head, not stretched, just...out of their way. It made no sense, but it seemed I wasn't supposed to have any control.

I *needed* to *feel.* Nothing else.

I was naked, the warm air moving lightly over my skin, cool against the wet heat of my open pussy. I was positioned like I was sitting in a chair, but there was no seat. My legs were spread wide to either side of my body, my thighs and most of my weight on a support I could not see, ass hanging out and over... a swing, open and bare. A swing? I didn't understand, but I didn't need to.

"Do you accept my claim, mate? Do you give yourself to me and my second freely, or do you wish to choose another primary male?" God, the growl in that voice almost made me come. My second mate stopped moving his fingers, his grip tightening, just enough, on my throat. My pussy clamped down on those fingers and I moaned. I needed *more.*

I licked my lips. "I accept your claim, warriors." And please fucking hurry! I knew they could feel my eagerness through our mating collars, the psychic connection linked us in a way I didn't understand. I could feel their need as if it were my own. Their desire. Possession.

Love.

God, yes, there was love there.

And just that fast, Erica Roberts of Earth didn't exist anymore. I gave in completely, sank deeper into the dream. *Felt.* I didn't want to leave this place, these warriors. This *feeling.* Not ever.

"Then I claim you in the rite of naming. You are mine, and I shall kill any other warrior besides my second who dares to touch you." My primary male spoke the vow with a voice I had never heard before, so solemn. He meant what he said. He would kill to protect me.

He stepped between my open thighs and my second mate removed his fingers from deep in my pussy, using the wet digits to spread my pussy lips, to open me up for his primary male's cock. As the first filled me, the mate at my back spoke his own vow. "You belong to us now. You are mine, and I am yours. I will die to protect you and our offspring. Kill to protect you. *Mine*. Forever, mate."

I cried out as the first male surged forward, his way eased by my eagerness and the assistance of my second. I was stretched open, filled. When he was fully seated, deep and thick, my secondary male moved his hand to my ass, pulling gently on the plug I hadn't noticed. How had I missed something so carnal? So... daring. It came free easily, and my second pushed his fingers deep into my ass. I gasped at the intrusion, of feeling so full. I'd never had someone even play with my ass, let alone fill it. Not with a small plug or a finger, but fingers. Plural.

I clenched down, breathed through the intensity of it.

I was wet there, whatever lubricant he had used working so well I all but begged him to start fucking me. I had no idea it could feel so good.

But I didn't want his fingers; I wanted his cock. I wanted both of them inside me. Deep. Together. Fucking me. Making me theirs. "Please. Please. I need you." I begged. I didn't care. They were mine, totally and completely mine. There was no shame in me, no holding back. "Pleeeease." I jerked against the bonds around my wrists, clamped down with my pussy muscles on the huge cock inside me.

The chanting stopped. I had all but forgotten our witnesses, too distracted by my mates to care about anything but *us*. "May the gods witness and protect you."

The words barely registered before the mate in front of me claimed my lips, kissing me like he wanted to devour me.

I wanted that too.

At the same time, my second mate positioned his cock at my back entrance, carefully but with intent, pushed forward, opened me. Filled me.

I groaned into the kiss, shifted my hips, tried to anyway, so I could rock back and forth. Fuck myself on their two hard cocks.

Too big, too much. More.

Instead, my first mate's hands clamped around my waist and he held me still. My second still had one hand around my throat, and I loved it, his other went to my breast, then nipple, squeezing. Tugging.

I was surrounded. Claimed. Safe. So full of cock I was going to scream if they didn't move. Now.

As if they realized they'd pushed me to the edge of sanity, they moved, both of them, pulling in and out together. Slowly. Fucking me together. Filling me up.

Sex felt good. Yeah, just good. *Usually.* For me anyway, regular old Erica from Earth.

In. Out. Rub. Stroke. Caress. Orgasms, when done by hand… literally, were good. There was that word again. That was because it *was* good. Just that.

Until now.

Until *this.*

Holy shit, THIS.

CHAPTER 3

Commander Karter, Battleship Varsten, Sector 438

"*R*onan? Fuck, I thought you were dead. Killed five years ago on Latiri 4."

My old friend stood, and I saw the ripped remains of his uniform, the blood on his temple and chest. He had not gone untouched in the battle, which meant he'd been on this ship when it had been attacked. Why had he been here, and why was he still here now? "Why did the Hive leave the dead? And how did you survive?"

He took a step toward me and Bard stepped between us, his ion rifle raised in his free hand. Ronan lifted his brows, a hardness I recognized in his golden eyes.

Ronan's arms slowly lifted out at his sides to show his hands were empty and he meant no threat. "Really? You're going to order him to shoot me?"

I didn't move, didn't even flinch. I'd seen things he couldn't imagine.

Or perhaps, he could.

"I haven't seen you in five years," I countered, tipping my chin up. No matter how pleased—and stunned—I was to find him alive, there had to be a reason for his disappearance. "You were reported killed in action on Latiri 4. You might be contaminated, controlled by the Hive, your mind not your own. You could be full of Hive implants. In which case, you wouldn't think twice about killing all of us and betraying your own people."

He nodded once. "Too true. I can't blame you, old friend, not after what just happened here." The fire left his gaze and he slumped back, sitting once more in the chair, ignoring the ion pistol pointed at him.

Bard lowered his weapon but didn't step back, remaining at the ready. With what surrounded us, we were all tense, all on guard, waiting for more destruction.

"What happened here, Ronan? How the fuck did the Hive get this close to a battleship?"

While any ship in a battlegroup was a potential target for Hive attack, no battleship had ever been hit this far inside Coalition space. Not like this. The standard orbital distance was—had been—too far for Hive weapons to be effective, our perimeter defenses and attack vessels making the main body of the fleet a difficult, if not impossible target. Until now.

Ronan ran his hand through his hair, inspecting the blood that clung to his palm as he lowered it. Stared at the dark stain. "They didn't get through the defense grid. Not one forward scout ship was attacked. There was no warning. No ships. Nothing. The Hive weren't even here, Kaed."

He called me by my nickname, one I hadn't heard in a long time. No one ever called me by my given name, Makaed. Not anymore. Not in years. That name belonged to an ambitious, hope-filled young Prillon male who had perished what felt like a lifetime ago.

"The I.C. knew the Hive were working on a long-range weapon of some sort, but we didn't know what it was. Or where it was."

I frowned, set my hands on my hips. "A long-range weapon? What are you talking about? There was nothing about a new threat in the command reports." Those reports came directly from Prillon Prime and were sent to the active fleet commanders every day, sometimes twice a day, depending on how hot the battlefields ran.

"This isn't the first attack. They took out the entire Battlegroup Hyrad ten days ago. Every single ship." Ronan shook his head. "The I.C. didn't have enough information to report or recommend any new course of action."

"What?" An entire battlegroup had been destroyed and I knew nothing of it? "You must tell the fleet commanders. First Hyrad and now Varsten. You are risking thousands of lives on the other battlegroups if you don't provide them with accurate intel." Rage boiled hot for the I.C. and their constant games. "I'm going to contact Prime Nial. You'll be executed for this."

"Prime Nial knows. He's the one who sent me here." He looked up at me, and this time there was regret in his eyes. The I.C. had fucked up, royally, and he knew it.

"Tell me you're lying. Why would he allow the I.C. to keep this from us?" Us, as in the commanders in the Coalition Fleet. The warriors responsible for protecting well over two hundred planets with billions of lives. Without consistent intel, we could do nothing to protect the people. This ship, this vessel that was barely holding together, was a perfect example of what could happen.

"He sent me here because they had intel that Varsten would be next. We hoped to lure the Hive into a trap."

I lost my temper, and I never lost my temper. I was across the room, Ronan's throat in my hand. When I lifted him, the

17

chair tipped over and I turned, pushed his back to the nearest wall. I lifted him off his feet and *squeezed.*

"Commander Karter." My second in command, Bard, placed his hand on my shoulder and pulled me back. Ronan was my oldest friend. We'd run the corridors of Battlegroup Karter when my grandfather had been in command of the ship. We'd sworn to be brothers, have each other's backs. He had pledged to be my second if I ever took a mate.

Thank the gods that had never happened, and never would. Not now. I'd been tested for a bride years ago. No bride had ever appeared, and I was confident none ever would. I was a damaged man, mated to battle. Mated to war. I lived, ate, and breathed to save my people, not to sacrifice them to some unknown Hive weapon. And yet, here we were, death and the leftovers of evil strewn at our feet.

I loosened my hold but did not release Ronan from my grasp. "Tell me every detail, and I might not kill you."

His face was a mottled purple and yet he smiled, but it held no humor. "Commander Varsten knew everything," he said, his voice deep, raspy from my hold. "He knew the risks and that's why he chose this ship as bait. That's why he was flying. He made the call. They all did. They stayed and we sent as many as we could into hiding."

Varsten knew his battleship was going to be attacked? I thought of the grizzled old Prillon commander. He'd raised two sons and a daughter, been mated for many years. He was stubborn as iron ore and impossible to break. If Ronan said he'd known, then he had. The risk would not have deterred him. And this information explained a few things. "Is that why most of his fleet is on the other side of this star system?"

Ronan nodded. "Varsten left the main battleship"—he waved his arm in the air to indicate this now-dead vessel —"to pilot an attack scout ship. He transported off all non-essential personnel after I arrived. All mates and children, civilians and medical staff. There was a skeleton crew on board these few forward ships. Maybe fifty warriors. Most of the ships were manned with pilots and weapons stations only. All volunteers. We told them everything, Kaed. We needed enough ships to bait the Hive into an attack."

I looked at Bard, my head spinning. He shrugged, obviously thinking. "It would explain the low number of fatalities, and the reason the Hive left the dead."

"The Hive were never here," Ronan said again. "Their strike came from the other side of the star. We weren't supposed to know what hit us."

"But you do?" I asked, setting him slowly onto his feet but not removing my hand from his throat. I felt the pulsing of his blood through the artery under my palm, felt his life force. After all these years, he really was alive. "Please tell me all these warriors did not die in vain, that Commander Varsten did not die for *nothing*."

"I don't know what it is, this weapon the Hive is using. But Commander Varsten sent out an I.C. probe in advance of the attack. It should have recorded everything from a safe distance."

"And where is this probe now?" I asked, my thoughts quickly spinning to the data that could be retrieved, data paid for with many lives lost.

He shrugged. "It's sitting at assigned coordinates, but not broadcasting. We'll need to send a stealth ship, small, fast, something the Hive won't bother looking for, to retrieve the probe. If we activate its quantum comms remotely, the Hive will blow it to pieces before we can access the data."

He was right. Whatever information was on the probe had to be retrieved at any cost, and yet very carefully. Commander Varsten had died for it. Nearly fifty brave warriors had been willing to sacrifice themselves to obtain the information. An entire battleship had been destroyed and was now just a floating wreck. Releasing him, I turned my back and put my helmet back on. "I fucking hate the I.C."

"It's war you hate, brother," Ronan said. "Not me."

His words held so much pain I could not ignore them. He was my brother in everything but blood. And he'd done his job. Just like I had to do mine. I looked at Bard, who lowered his weapon. "Get the rest of Varsten's fleet on the move. Confirm they're out of range of whatever this weapon is before we lose more people."

Bard nodded. "What about you, Commander?"

I looked at Ronan. "We have a probe to hunt."

Bard opened his mouth to protest, but I raised my hand to stall the argument I knew was coming. "Get back to the Karter. I need you there. We're going to have incoming crew, ships and defenses to coordinate. I have a feeling we're going to have to stretch our resources over both sectors. Prime Nial won't want to abandon this sector. It's too close to populated planets. We'll have to hold it. And we need to report this to the rest of the fleet commanders."

"No. Not until we know what we're dealing with." Ronan ignored three of my men who came into the room, probably ready for new orders to fulfill. They pointed their weapons at him, an unknown. Ronan ignored them all and came to me, standing toe-to-toe. "Give me twelve hours. I'll have that probe and we'll have some answers."

I stared into the eyes of the man I'd loved like a brother, whose death I had mourned more than all but my own father's. And I hated him for knowingly putting lives in danger, knowing an attack was imminent, and sacrificing those warriors anyway. Hated that he'd disappeared, *died,* and then returned. Hated him for knowing too many secrets. For saying whatever he had to convince Commander Varsten to fly straight into a Hive trap.

Fuck.

"Get that probe. If all of these warriors died for nothing, Ronan, I'll kill you myself."

"If this was for nothing, we're all dead anyway," he countered, his voice grim.

The finality of his words sent ice-cold dread through my veins. I knew this man, knew how strong he'd always been. He was a brilliant battle strategist and as tough as they came. I'd never been afraid of dying, but he didn't speak of death. He spoke of annihilation, and worse. Assimilation. Loss of self. Billions of lives on hundreds of worlds falling prey to the Hive menace we'd fought for centuries.

Until now, I'd never once feared we might not win this war. And fear was a sensation I did not want to feel again. "Get the fucking probe. Then we'll talk."

He nodded just as a buzzing sounded in the ship's systems.

"Commander Karter, this is Battleship Karter. Please respond."

"This is Karter," I barked into my helmet.

"Sir, you need to get to the transport room as quickly as possible for an incoming transport."

I looked at Bard, who shook his head. We were in agreement.

"I told you, no incoming transports. This ship is running on power reserves and is still in danger." When the voice through the comms remained silent, I continued, "Explain. The Varsten has been attacked. The entire battlegroup has been compromised. The ship is not safe for non-essential personnel. Again, no one is to come here but warriors or medical crew, as ordered."

"I understand, Commander, but the transport system is still operational. My apologies, I couldn't stop them."

Couldn't stop who? "What are you talking about? Get to the point. I'm busy."

"I tried to stop them, sir, but it was too late."

"Too late?" As a commander I had learned to dread those words. "Too late to stop what?"

"Your bride, Commander. The Interstellar Brides Program on Earth pinged your location via the transport system and initiated transport to Battleship Varsten automatically. Your bride is mid-transport. I cannot reroute her without risking her life."

"My what?" My mind refused to process his words. It simply was not possible.

"Your Interstellar Bride, Commander. Congratulations, sir. She will arrive in the next few minutes."

CHAPTER 4

Erica Roberts, Interstellar Brides Processing Center, Earth

*I*t was like I was a sex goddess and they worshipped me.

This was like the *Hallelujah* chorus and a porno combined with lots and lots of wine. I was relaxed and sweaty, and there were multiple hands and mouths and cocks. A mouth was sucking on my nipple. A cock was buried deep in my pussy, filling me just shy of too much. *I had a cock fucking my ass.*

I realized the strange whimpering sound I heard was *me.*

"Easy, mate," the deep voice said. "We'll give you what you need."

Oh good, because I needed to come. Really hard and right now. I'd never been this wound up, this... passion-filled. Aggressive. Desperate. Out of control.

Oh my god. No wonder sex had only been good before. I'd been missing out... on an extra man.

I couldn't see him. Either of them. I didn't care. It was a

dream, I knew. A fabulous dream I never, ever wanted to wake up from. At least until they made me come. And they would.

"More. Harder." Was that my voice all breathy and forceful?

When hands gripped my hips and a cock drove into me just as I'd requested, I cried out, the sound mixing with the slapping of flesh on flesh.

"When you come, mate," the voice belonged to the mate behind me, the other one was too busy claiming my mouth, shutting me up, swallowing my cries of pleasure. "Your pussy will milk the cum from his cock. It will mark you as his and fill you up so there's no chance you aren't bred." Another nip to my shoulder and I gasped. "You will wake in the morning with our baby growing in your belly."

I—she—writhed. *A baby?*

Did I want that? This woman did. God did she, the dirty talk was getting me—her—closer and closer to the brink. And yet, it wasn't me. *This* wasn't me. The woman was someone else, these mates, they belonged to *her*. They weren't mine, but I was feeling their desire, sharing their pleasure. Knowing how good it would be with my own mates. It was as if I'd taken over their sexy times. As if it were an interactive porno.

The hands on my hips tightened almost painfully as the pace of fucking intensified. My primary mate broke off the kiss to rumble in my ear. "Don't worry, my balls are so full of cum for you. We'll be at you all night if that's what it takes. You want my baby, mate. The collars don't lie. I'm going to fill you up with seed. You're ours, mate. Come for us, take what you want, take it all."

I did, the orgasm so intense I couldn't scream, couldn't move, my muscles tense. Taut. The cock pistoned inside me as I did milk it, trying to take it impossibly deeper, to keep it inside me as if it belonged there. I needed his seed, his claim, his baby.

I heard the growl of possessiveness as he came. I felt the heat of his cum as he filled me. It went on and on, as if his pleasure was as intense as mine.

Behind me, my second mate came as well, filling my ass full of his seed, too, marking me just as thoroughly as his counterpart.

I gasped, jerking as aftershocks ripped through me. I wanted more. More orgasms, more kisses. More. Just *more.*

Instead, they faded, their touch as they kept fucking me becoming less intense. The heat was gone. Then the pressure. No more cocks filling me up. No more hands. I couldn't hear them anymore and the link to them faded until I was alone in my head again.

Alone. As usual.

But now I knew what I was missing, and the lonely emptiness in my body hit me with ten times the normal cold because I'd been so hot just seconds ago.

"No." A meager protest, based on the dry whisper that managed to sneak its way out of my throat, but I had to protest. I wanted to go back. I wanted to be wanted like that. Needed. Lusted after. Loved.

"Ms. Roberts, your testing is complete."

That voice. Damn it, I knew that voice, but I didn't want to come back. I wanted to stay with my mates. "My mates." I hated the choking pain I heard in my own voice, but I couldn't stop the protest. No one had ever touched me like that, made me feel like I was his, no their, world.

"All in good time, Ms. Roberts." That matter-of-fact tone brought me fully back to reality, and I recognized the firm press of the testing chair beneath me. This place, it was like going to the dentist, a necessary evil. But this was no ordinary dentist's chair. I was locked down, wrists, waist and ankles secured with padded buckles like I was some kind of dangerous criminal.

But then, sometimes the women in this chair *were* criminals. Just not me. I was a volunteer. I had nothing left on this rock called Earth. After I'd caught my ex-fiancé sleeping with my roommate, I'd dumped his ass and taken the new job at the observatory on the big island of Hawaii, thinking the stars I loved so much would distract me from what a low-life loser I'd almost married.

Instead, those small twinkling lights had called to me. I had been staring up at the stars for almost as long as I could remember, the obsession never leaving me, not even when I graduated after finishing my master's and started my career in astronomy. Fifteen years ago, when I'd gotten my first telescope for my birthday, actually going *out there* hadn't been an option. There was no space travel. No aliens. Nothing. We'd been alone in the universe.

But now? Now we humans knew the truth. Earth was one of almost three hundred planets being protected by the Interstellar Coalition Fleet. Without the Coalition, Earth would fall prey to the Hive, a scary-as-fuck race of freakish biosynthetic cyborgs that consumed new races and new planets to feed their never-ending need to expand. Grow. Conquer.

They reminded me of the Borg from *Star Trek*, but I kept that opinion to myself at the office. Hell, everywhere. Half of the people thought the whole thing was a hoax and conspiracy to convince humanity to send sacrificial lambs up into space for freakish alien breeding programs, or as expendable soldiers for nothing but suicide missions.

I didn't believe the conspiracy theory websites. Not just because my mother was a NASA engineer and knew more about what was going on than most, but because there were a handful of warriors who'd come home after serving their two years. I'd made a point of tracking them down, reading their interviews, visiting as many as I could, as many as would talk to me. I wanted to know about the other worlds. What sort of animals roamed these unknown planets? What type of plants and terrain would I see? What did the aliens who populated those worlds look like? What did they eat? What were their customs? I wanted to know everything.

But all they ever talked about was war. PTSD on a massive scale. Whatever was out there, it was bad. Those who *would* talk to me—once I used my own university credentials to convince them I was not a fanatic or an all-around crazy person—talked of little but the battlefields, and the enemy.

As terrifying as the Hive sounded, I wanted to know everything. But I wanted to know how the other Coalition races *lived,* not just how they died. War was war. It sucked. But what were all those alien warriors fighting to protect?

Guess I'd find out, assuming the testing had worked. I sure as hell hoped it had. I was not small, which my ex had taken great pleasure in pointing out as often as possible. I was tall to start with, as tall as a lot of men, and yes—I was carrying a bit of extra weight. But I loved my body. The softness of my stomach, my extra-large breasts. Skinny girls didn't get the goods, and I had them in spades. Boobs. Ass. Boom-baby. I didn't want to go home, back to work, back to my *normal* life. I would never be the same again, not after this. Not after *them.* The two mates in the dream. They weren't mine, but still. Wow.

Now I was addicted, needed two men, two cocks. Dirty talk and four hands and hard, hot fucking. Lots and lots of cum that would make me—

Shit.

"Ms. Roberts? Can you hear me?" She sounded impatient now, the woman I could sense looming over me. She wasn't

27

mean, just... efficient. I wanted to linger in that magical place, stuffed full of two hard cocks and more love than I'd ever felt in my entire...

"Erica, do you need a doctor?"

Damn. "No. I'm fine." I opened my eyes and blinked, taking in the testing room. Sweat coated my skin, the orgasm that had been just a dream lingered, my skin warm, my nipples hard, my heart racing.

But was it all about the sex?

No, my mind would not let go of exactly what those warriors had promised to their mate. Cum. Seed. Baby.

On Earth, I couldn't even find a man who wanted to have sex with me. Those who weren't afraid of my height were freaked the fuck out by my...

"Erica, are you sure you're all right?" Warden Egara asked, coming to stand before me. "You're taking a bit longer than usual to come out of the testing phase."

Testing phase? Was that what they called intense orgasms around here?

"Sorry, I just didn't want to come back yet. It was just getting good." Liar-liar-pants on fire.

"Perfectly understandable. Your match is exceptional. Ninety-nine percent."

Thank god. I didn't have to go back to my old life. Which was a good thing, since I'd already sold all my stuff and my roommate had rented out my bedroom for nearly twice what I'd been paying. Highly unlikely she'd want me back.

"So, I got a good match?" Small trembles shook my arms, then moved to my legs. The utilitarian hospital-style gown I wore didn't offer much in the heat department. And it *was* Florida, but that just meant the air conditioning was on full throttle and warm-blooded creatures like me needed winter coats and blankets to survive indoors, even if I'd lived in Hawaii the past few years.

"Oh, yes. You've been matched to Prillon Prime." Her smile was genuine, if a bit sad. "It happens to be my personal favorite."

"You've been there? Out there?" Holy shit. Had this woman actually been to outer space?

"Yes. I was mated to two Prillon warriors myself. Years ago."

Years ago? She didn't look all that old. Maybe thirty. Close to my age. Her dark hair was pulled back in a severe bun, but it only showed off how pretty she was. The dark gray of the IBP uniform did nothing for her, but it wasn't as if she'd go to the bar with girlfriends while wearing it. Before the testing I had wondered if she was married, dating anyone. Now I wanted to know more about her mates, but didn't ask. If she was here, and they weren't, I had a feeling the answer wouldn't be good.

"So why were there two mates?" I knew there were two, from my dream, but I was eager for an explanation. And she had just confirmed that she'd had two mates as well.

"The males of Prillon Prime are warriors, usually on the front lines of the fight. Most of the time they keep their brides with them on whichever battleship they serve. The warriors live most of their lives in space. They always claim a mate in pairs in case one of them is killed in battle. That way the surviving male can either choose another second, if their female agrees, or retire and move his family to Prillon Prime. Either way, one mate remains to care for his female and children."

"That explains the two men in my dream."

She looked up at me and gave me a wink, which made me blush. "Rather fabulous, wasn't it?"

Forget blush, I was bright red now, the heat like a blowtorch under my cheeks. "Well, it was nice, but two?" My grandmother would roll over in her grave and start praying

Hail Mary's all over the place. I was going to hell. Straight. To. Hell.

Or Prillon Prime.

"You don't sound excited about that." The Interstellar Brides Program logo was repeated across the fabric of her uniform, not that I could forget where I was. Even though I was restrained to the chair, I tugged at the secure hold.

I arched a brow. "Two mates? I… I never thought about it before. I guess I knew it was a possibility, I mean, I've heard that brides who go to Viken have three men."

"Three mates. They are not human, Ms. Roberts. But that's right." Her grin widened, but she looked down at her tablet to hide her reaction to my comment. "Three. Can you just imagine."

Lord help me, I *could.* Which was not good. I was desperate to get back into the middle of a Prillon man-sandwich as quickly as possible. I didn't need her asking me questions about where my head was right now, because I didn't know. My vagina seemed to be in charge. And I didn't want to think about the wetness soaking the gown under my ass. Or the little jolts of electricity still zinging through my pussy at random intervals. My ass, too.

"I just need to ask you a few questions before I can begin your processing."

"Shoot."

"I must make sure you are aware of your rights, Ms. Roberts. This will be recorded." She stared at me, an impatient tilt to her head, eyes wide open as if to hurry me along.

"I understand."

"Excellent. Ms. Roberts, as an Interstellar Bride, you may name a world, if you wish, and we will choose your mate from that world based on your assessment results. Or you may waive the right of naming and accept the results of the psychological assessment process. If you choose this option, you will be sent to the world, and the mate, that best matches your psychological profile. If you wish to meet your true mate, I highly recommend you choose the second option and follow the recommendations of the matching processors. We have been matching brides and their mates for hundreds of years."

"Okay." When I didn't say more, she pursed her lips but continued.

"Are you currently married?"

"No."

"Do you have any biological or adopted children you would be leaving behind?"

"No." To have kids, first you had to find someone willing to...

"State your name for the record, please."

"Erica Elaine Roberts."

"Good. Good." Her fingers flew over the tablet as we talked, as if she were checking off boxes for an exam. Seemed even aliens had bureaucracies and lots of red tape. "I am pleased to tell you, Ms. Roberts, that the system has made a successful match, and you will be sent to Battleship Varsten to meet your mate and I assume, his second. As a bride, you might never return to Earth, as all travel will be determined and controlled by your new planet's laws and customs. You now surrender your citizenship of Earth and become an official citizen of your new world."

Holy shit, now *I* was officially an alien?

I glanced down at my body, at the excess of curves and softness that no one seemed to want and figured what the hell? I felt like an alien half the time already. "I understand."

The wall began to glow with a beautiful blue behind me, the light casting the warden's face in shadows the seemed to haunt her somehow. Yet she still smiled. "You will have thirty days to decide if the primary candidate is acceptable. If, after

31

thirty days, you are not satisfied with your mate, you will be assigned another mate on that world and transferred. You will have thirty days to accept or reject each candidate until you are satisfied with a mate."

If they were anything like the males in my dream, there would be no need to trade them in for new ones. I'd be *well* satisfied. I couldn't wait. "Okay." That, it seemed, was my word of the day.

Warden Egara nudged the side of my chair and it slid toward the wall where a large opening appeared. I moved, chair and all, as if on a track, right into the newly revealed space on the other side of the wall.

The blue room was small and glowed, the color coming from streams of bright blue lights. My chair came to a stop and a robotic arm with a large needle moved silently closer to my neck. I winced as something pierced my skin.

Right. The NPU, or neural processing unit I read about in the handbook. A kind of universal translation thing that would make it so I could talk to my mates. Tell them what I wanted.

Where to touch me.

Wouldn't do me any good to beg if they didn't understand what I was saying.

Maybe I should get two of them. "How long does it take this translation thing to work?" I asked, speaking loudly because now Warden Egara was in the other room and everything was getting fuzzy.

"You might get a headache, but your transport is some distance. The NPU should be fully integrated prior to your arrival."

Sweet. Meet hot, sexy aliens. Make them fall madly in love and claim me forever. No problem.

Unless they didn't like big, beautiful women from Earth.

Or smart women. Or opinionated women. Or tall women. Or women who don't like to be treated like a doormat.

Then I was screwed.

The injection site tingled and a sense of lethargy and contentment made my body go limp. There had been more than just an alien computer chip in that injection. Drugs? Good drugs. Something was making me very, very sleepy and happy. But whatever. I felt too good to worry about it as I was lowered into a bath of warm blue liquid. I was so warm, so numb...

"Relax, Erica. You're going to a good place." Her finger touched the display in her hand, and her voice drifted to me as if from far, far away. "Your processing will begin in three... two... one..."

CHAPTER 5

Commander Ronan Wothar, Intelligence Core, Sector 438, Battleship Varsten

"You shouldn't be here, Karter. And no female should be either. It's too fucking dangerous." By the gods, it really was Makaed Karter, my childhood friend, and possibly the only person in the universe who could recognize me after all these years. Old instincts surged. He was my friend, closer than my own brother when we'd been young.

Rubbing my throat in annoyance, I looked from Karter to his companion. The Prillon warrior standing at his side had the markings of the second in command on his uniform. "You should have stopped him. That's your job, Second. To protect him. Get him the hell off this ship. Now. I'll send your mate directly, after she arrives."

"You are in no position to issue orders, Ronan." Commander Karter's voice brooked no argument. "And I will not leave an innocent female here, mate or not."

"Still an arrogant ass, I see." I taunted him, knowing his honor would keep him in check. I expected no less from Makaed Karter. The perfect son. The perfect warrior. And now, no doubt, the perfect commander. He'd held a very dangerous sector of space against a very aggressive enemy for years. I read the reports, kept up on his battlegroup. I knew exactly who I was dealing with.

And fuck, though I knew he shouldn't be here, it was good to see a familiar face. A face that knew me, the real me. Not the I.C. *asset* who lived without any identification, who was considered just shy of rogue. While I'd volunteered for the secretive intelligence gathering group, there was no fucking way I'd have done it if I'd known how... alone I would become. Cut off.

I turned to the control panel and resumed scanning the data, looking for the probe, for the Hive ship. Something. Anything. There had to be something here, some clue. A trail. A hint of what the Hive had hit us with. There had to be.

"Why did you let me believe you were dead, Ronan? You were my brother."

There was no pain in his voice, but I felt it regardless. I knew the depths of the warrior who spoke to me. But what could I say? I lied to you because I made a huge mistake and joined the I.C.?

No. That would be a lie. I would have done it anyway. The Intelligence Core was the reason the Interstellar Coalition had made great progress in the war with the Hive. *That* was worth any sacrifice. That was worth the price I had paid. I had told myself that too many times to count. I could not stop believing it now just because we'd lost another battleship, a brilliant, seasoned commander and still had no idea what the fuck kind of weapon had been used against us. Two steps forward, one giant fucking leap backward.

"I did what needed to be done, same as you."

He grunted at my words but turned and walked away, most likely heading toward the transport room to greet his new bride.

I watched him go, my gut churning with conflicting instincts. Stay. Follow him. Let him go. Claim the female and demand my place as his second.

Nothing was easy. Nothing could be done without fighting someone, whether it was Karter, the I.C. or myself.

A few months ago, my superior officers at Core Command had been sitting around with huge smiles on their faces, congratulating each other and patting themselves on the back. A Nexus unit had been taken down, the first, but not by a member of the Intelligence Core, or by a fleet commander, but by a human cyborg female sent to the Colony, and by her new mate, a brute who, technically, wasn't even part of the Coalition, a Forsian from Rogue 5, a bastard the size of an Atlan and twice as mean.

How those two had taken down the Nexus was still a matter of debate. The female and her mate had stolen a ship soon after and disappeared, leaving a group of dead Hive Soldiers, a dead Hive Integration Unit, and the body of the Nexus himself rotting in a cave beneath Colony Base 3.

Dissecting the Nexus had earned us a deeper understanding of how their biology was formed. Prior to that, only one other Nexus unit had been killed, again by a human female, Captain Megan Simmons, and her mate, Nyko, an Atlan with a mean streak and a bad attitude. Before the I.C. even knew the captain had been successful in acquiring a neural transmission junction from the spine of the Nexus unit on Latiri 4, the Hive had removed their dead.

We had the Nexus' helmet, and the disgusting wormlike neural unit—still squirming and searching for brains—somewhere on ice in the vaults at Core Command. Doctor Helion and the rest of the I.C. science teams had spent countless hours trying to understand the Hive physiology, with little luck.

It seemed the Nexus and the rest of the Hive we battled were completely different. The Hive soldiers were biological hijackings, bodies of conquered people they'd taken form other worlds and contaminated with their synthetic technology.

But the Nexus themselves were a different species entirely, something we'd never seen before.

The body from the Colony had given them more information, but still not enough.

And now this.

Two battlegroups destroyed in less than two weeks. At this rate, the Hive would overrun the entire Coalition Fleet in a matter of weeks.

The I.C. was currently hunting for the Forsian and his female. They were the only warriors known to have successfully tracked and killed a Nexus unit. They had answers we needed, but they had vanished, and Governor Maxim of Base 3 claimed not to know much. But then, he was Prillon, with a human mate of his own, and she had been as tight-lipped as her two mates.

I'd met Earth females, Captain Megan Simmons among them. They were tough and liked to keep their secrets. If Governor Maxim claimed not to know how the human female—now cyborg—had tracked the Nexus unit, I believed him.

Damn stubborn females. She most likely needed a good spanking and a good fucking, in that order. But to do that, I'd have to get past the Forsian monster who'd claimed her for his own.

Damn near impossible, even if the I.C. knew where to find them.

Still, a tempting prospect. Human females were all softness and curves, usually with a feisty mouth to go with them. Everything I wanted in a female, and I'd admired the few I'd run into.

I wondered if Karter's mate would have soft, dark skin like Megan, or be a light brown color more like I.C. Commander Chloe Phan? Perhaps she'd be fair and golden like Kira, the bride I'd met on the Colony, mated to the Warlord Anghar, or fair of skin but dark haired like Governor Maxim's female, Rachel.

I'd spent several weeks on the Colony and my admiration for Earth females had only grown from interest to obsession. I wanted one for myself.

The Hive's interest in the Colony had been our main focus the last few months, until the Hyrad had been destroyed, and now the Varsten. The Hive had a new weapon, a game-changing, win the war and wipe out the entire Interstellar Coalition, weapon.

I'd been sent here to find out what it was and how it worked, so we could stop it. All I'd done so far was get good warriors killed.

I needed that probe. And I prayed to the gods there was valuable information contained on its database, something we could use to counter or destroy their new weapon.

If not, we were doomed. And so were my old friend and his new bride.

That was not acceptable to me. Knowing his bride would be arriving from Earth made me doubly determined to protect them both. No doubt she would be soft and curvy, sassy and submissive. Perfect. Matched to Makaed Karter, she could be nothing less.

And I would have been his second, the pledge made years ago when we'd been not yet twenty, running the corridors of the battleship, playing at war. Karter and I had been closer than brothers then. We'd longed to attend the Coalition

Academy, to test our mettle. Wet behind the ears and so fucking young. We'd both excelled, worked our way up the ranks until we earned our own commands.

And now Karter had a whole fucking battlegroup answering to him. He was known. *Very* known in the Coalition. Infamous. Then there was me, his best friend. I'd hit captain, then taken a sharp left at I.C., worked my up to commander, and there had been no path back.

My superiors had faked my death and erased my records in case the Hive ever caught me. Obviously, I wasn't dead, but in the eyes of the Coalition, I'd been lost in a battle five years earlier. Body taken by the Hive, destination unknown. Plausible, since that was what happened to almost every fighter lost on Latiri 4 if they were not lucky enough to be retrieved by one of our own.

No one questioned my death. No one missed me. And so I fought, in my own stealth way, in a way few had. I didn't exist. I could blend in, become whatever my superiors wanted. Mission after mission. And since I was already dead, they didn't have to worry if something ever happened to me. I didn't kid myself. I wasn't irreplaceable. I was *valuable*, but that was it.

And now, holy fuck. Now, seeing Karter, those five years were blown. I existed again. Someone knew me. Knew everything important about me. I hadn't cared for so long, but seeing my friend made the need to… belong, rush back. And when he'd discovered he'd been matched, that his mate was arriving here, on this wreck, I had a purpose again. Something more than battling a never-ending enemy.

Years ago, I'd vowed to be his second. I'd been serious then, and I was serious now. Fate had set me on the same ship as Karter at this time. I was meant to be his second, to protect the female we would both love, and I would not take my responsibility lightly.

I would not turn away from this, and I would not allow Kaed Karter to deny me what was mine. Our female. Our mate. He obviously needed someone to knock some sense into that thick skull, and I would not deny my responsibility. I didn't want to.

Standing, I left the console and made my way to the transport room. There, I walked in with purpose. Injured were lined up awaiting their turn at being sent to a viable ship with a med unit. With ReGen pods to heal them.

Karter turned at my entrance, came around the wounded being tended on the floor. "I thought you'd be off collecting the data from the probe, then off to I.C."

I shook my head, clenching my fists as a wounded fighter was carried up to the transport pad, then disappeared. The vibrations of the transport buzzed beneath my feet, but I was so used to the electrical current in the air, the hairs on my body no longer stood on end.

"I await our mate," I said plainly.

Karter's dark eyes widened and he set his hands on his hips. It might have been five years since I'd seen him last, but I knew him well. Remembered the intensity, his focus. "*Our* mate?"

"You asked me to be your second and I accepted, Kaed. Vows were made. Do you deny it?"

"That was before you died."

I paused. "Have you chosen another as your second?" I asked. The strange sensation of... hurt swelled in my chest.

"Fuck you, Ronan."

I knew it. Even with me dead, he'd been too damn stubborn to break his oath to me. "I'm your second, Commander. And since your weak-willed second in command allowed you to set foot on this ship, you clearly need me to help you protect our female."

"She's not mine. I was tested years ago. I don't have time

for a mate. My life is not suited for a female. Fuck, look where we are! This ship is barely holding together. One small meteor bouncing off the exterior shields and it might crumple. Blown to bits by an unknown Hive weapon." He raised his arm indicating the others around us. Injured. Proof of how evil the Hive could be. "And she's coming *here*. Why would the Brides Program match an innocent, from *Earth*, to be mine? This is my life."

His words rang true. He was a battlegroup commander. Important. Valuable. And always in the thick of danger.

"We will not remain on this ship. She will be safe on Battleship Karter."

"Will she? Varsten is dead and he knew this... weapon was aiming right for him. You said Battlegroup Hyrad was blown to bits last week. The *entire* battlegroup. Thousands are dying and yet I have a mate arriving in the thick of it."

"We will protect her."

He tried to smile, but it looked more a sneer. "And you? Her second? A member of the I.C. so stealthy you don't even exist. How can you be her second; how will you protect her, if you aren't here, if you exist only as a ghost? A dead man?"

I reached down, cupped my cock. "I assure you, I am very much alive. I am a commander, Kaed, equal in rank to you. And she will not doubt that when we claim her."

"We are a danger to her."

Thank fuck he'd used the word *we*. "We do not know why she comes. Her reasons for being a bride. Is she fleeing danger on Earth? Was a male harming her? Does she seek protection from two males? She needs what only you can give her if she was matched to you."

Slowly, he shook his head, let his hands fall to his sides. The hum of the transport picked up again, and I glanced up as another wounded fighter disappeared. Within a second, he'd be with the med techs on Battleship Karter, getting the help he needed.

"We aren't safe. We are a danger to her. And with you off on missions, she will not have two mates to satisfy her. Protect her. How can you say you'll be her second if you won't be there to keep her safe if something happens to me? And it will. It is only a matter of time."

I stepped closer, set my hand on his shoulder, looked my friend in the eye in a way I hadn't done in a half a decade. "She is coming here. She is yours. You will solve this like you solve all problems."

He stepped back. "Exactly. A problem. What female wants to be a mate who is considered a *problem?*"

"Commander," the transport tech called. "Your mate is arriving next. We have paused transporting the injured for her arrival."

Kaed gave me a knowing look. A mate complicated everything. Delayed the remaining injured from getting the help they needed. It wasn't her fault. She had no control of being sent from Earth. It was the Interstellar Brides Program that sent mates when matched.

"I want her. I vowed to be your second and I will not renege on that. It may have been five years since we've seen each other last, but my honor has not changed. Nor has yours."

The vibration began again. This time, we turned to look at the platform. It was empty and before our eyes, *she* appeared. Sprawled across the metal surface, she looked like one of the injured, except for no blood. Unconscious.

And, as I had dreamed, very soft. Curved. And very, very naked.

Before my eyes, Karter's spine straightened. His chest puffed out and his gaze darkened. He was on the platform in two steps, I right behind.

Kaed seemed as stunned as I, staring at our female. She was tall, much taller than Commander Phan. The I.C. commander was small, compact with dark hair nearly black and a tight, compact body.

Not our female. She was tall with golden hair that curled at the ends and lush curves that would fill my hands. Large, full breasts with pink nipples, round, curved ass and full, soft thighs. Her stomach curved in a delightful softness I could not wait to fill with our seed and watch grow. She was lush. Soft.

Perfect.

My cock thought so as well, swelling to painful hardness in my pants.

Karter still hadn't moved, his dark hands a stark contrast to her fair flesh where he wrapped his arms around her.

"Commander, we need to clear the pad." The transport tech spoke softly, but the reprimand was there. We were staring, wasting time, delaying the transport of the injured.

"She's mine," Karter murmured as he lifted her easily into his arms and carried her down the steps, out of the way of the line of injured.

"Ours," I added when I stroked her silky hair back from her sleeping face. I was no longer dead. I was now a second in a Prillon life match. I now had a mate. I was alive and had a new mission.

Her.

CHAPTER 6

Erica

"*She's mine.*"

I heard a deep voice growl those words. It was as if I were in another testing dream, floating, not quite sleeping... hovering. I was laid out, not in the dentist chair from the processing center, but as if in a bed. It was the hardest bed I'd ever felt. Cold, too. More like a floor.

"Ours." A different voice, but no less gruff.

I felt large hands on me, lifting me to a somewhat upright position.

I couldn't see—I wasn't fully awake—but I could hear. A variety of sounds came to me. The two men weren't alone. I heard other voices, but farther away. All clear, urgent. Banging of metal, as if a hammer hitting a car. Bursts of air, like truck brakes being released.

Soft fabric was pushed over my head. Warm and the scent of... of something I didn't recognize. Dark. Appealing. I took a deep breath and blinked, saw flashes of light. Color.

Blinked again.

Hands were on me, moving mine, slipping my arms into sleeves of a dark shirt. The hands were tanned, corded tendons, thick veins. The size of dinner plates.

"Commander, the next transport sequence has been accepted. Please move clear of the transport pad."

I was lifted easily—too easily for a woman of my size—and I was moving, down a few steps, then lowered into someone's lap.

I lifted my head. Blinked once more. A man—no, not a man, an alien—was kneeling before me. I had to tilt my chin back to look at his face. It hadn't felt as if I'd been transported off Earth, but just looking at him, I knew.

I wasn't on Earth any longer. He was looking at me, his gaze roving over every inch of me. Intent, focused, sharp.

The eyes were dark, like chocolate, the same color as his hair. But his skin had the most amazing tan, as if he lived in Florida and spent all his time outdoors. He looked like a man from Earth, but... more. Bigger, like supersized. With him kneeling, I couldn't tell how tall he was, but his shoulders were broad and I had to wonder if they'd fill a doorway. Muscles bulged beneath his black shirt. He was... hot. God, like seriously, incredibly gorgeous. And all of his attention was focused squarely on me.

"Mate, are you well?"

The voice was like rocks tumbling down a stream. Deep. Mesmerizing. He continued to study me as I remained silent, but realized he was waiting. While he seemed patient, tension vibrated from him. I sensed anger, frustration and other things I didn't understand.

"Yes, I'm fine." I looked down, saw I'd been covered in a similar black shirt as his, and yet the one I wore had definitely seen better days. But a few rips and... oh God, what looked suspiciously like blood… was better than remaining naked in front of total strangers.

The arms about me tightened, then began to rove over me. My arms, my shoulders, the back of my neck, then back down. I was sitting in someone's lap, not *his,* felt the warmth of the second person where I was pressed against him. My shoulder in his hard chest—where his heartbeat was steady—and lower, my hip pressing into his… oh shit.

Was that his cock? It felt like the proverbial pipe in his pants. Thick, long, hard.

"You transported a long way," the voice by my ear murmured. Oh, this other voice was deep, delicious. "No headaches, nausea…"

I turned my head and looked up at him. Wow. There were two hotties. This one was a surfer god… all tousled blond hair, golden streaks as if out in the ocean and sun all day. His coloring was similar to the other, but his eyes… like caramel.

Warden Egara had said I'd been matched to Prillon Prime, which meant these men were Prillons. And like the dream, there were two of them. She'd actually said, "You're going to a good place."

I believed her now. I could see why she said I'd be happy. Why the woman in the testing dream had been in heaven in the middle of a sexy man sandwich.

He, too, was waiting for me to respond. I shook my head. No pain. No unsettled stomach. I *was* a little sleepy, but I didn't want to close my eyes or sleep. I wanted to look at these two all day long. "No, I'm fine."

I might have been on another planet, but it only felt like ten minutes since I'd spoken with Warden Egara, her telling me the testing had been successful. The same amount of time since the dream. Since I'd come. Hard. My body was still lethargic and sated from that. My pussy still felt achy and tender, as if the dream had been real. My nipples were pebbled beneath the borrowed shirt because arousal still lingered.

I wasn't unwell. I was horny. But I didn't say that to either of them.

"We need to get her off this ship. Now." The one whose lap I was in spoke again, his words clipped, his deep voice vibrating through my entire body and straight to my core. I nearly moaned, but bit back that response and replaced it with a soft sigh, burrowing deeper. This warrior was mine, too. I just knew it. If his hands softly stroking my skin weren't signal enough, when I turned around to face him, my eyes widened as I saw his bare chest. I was wearing his shirt. It smelled like him.

And I was naked beneath, the cool air flowing over bare skin under the heavy garment. Obviously, the hospital gown outfit I'd been wearing during testing didn't make it through transport.

The tanned coloring of his skin wasn't a tan at all. It was his natural skin tone. Every single well-defined muscle was visible, rippling as he moved, as he breathed. And the huge, naked chest I leaned against was pure, raw seduction. My mind went weird because all I could think about was trying to bounce a quarter off those abs. I wanted to lick him. Bite him. Taste him. I'd never seen muscles like this. Ever.

No doubt, the brooding warrior leaning over me like a dark angel would be just as freakishly hot with his shirt off. But he wasn't touching me. Hell, he stared at me like I was a bug under glass, a puzzle to be figured out.

A problem to be solved.

"No. She will remain, for now. The injured must go first." My dark-haired warrior's voice sounded angry, not at all pleased to meet me. Which wasn't how this was supposed to go down. They were supposed to see me, want me, claim me.

Hot sex and heat and perfect matches. That's what I was expecting.

But as I blinked away my hot sex, orgasm fueled transport haze to look around, I noticed new sounds.

Groans of pain.

Cursing—and thanks to the handy NPU Warden Egara had put in my head, I could understand all of it—in every language.

The smell of burnt flesh and blood wasn't strong enough to make me sick, but it was there, hovering like the stink of charred weeds from a days-old ditch fire.

What the hell? I craned my neck to see, but the dark warrior shifted position, blocking my attempts to see what was going on behind him. Big freaking shoulders? Yeah. Too big, at the moment.

"Injured? What? Who's hurt?" I asked, tensing. The big hand from my golden mate began to rove over me again, up and down my back, as if to soothe me.

"Get her out of here, Kaed." The stroke of his hand was gentle, but the male who touched me sounded far from tender. "Now. She can't be here."

"I just got here. Why do you want to get rid of me?" I asked them both.

"This ship is not safe. It has been under Hive attack." Kaed. That was his name. The dark, brooding sex god who looked good enough to eat. *Thank you, Warden Egara...*

"But you are here," I countered. "I am your mate. I go where you go."

"No. You do not."

"Yes, I do. That's how this mate thing works." Duh. I could write it out in big, elementary school sized, block letters for him if he needed me to.

Behind me, the hot chest I leaned against chuckled. "Earth females. I knew she would be feisty."

Feisty? They hadn't seen anything yet. I'd show them fucking feisty. I did not travel halfway across the flipping universe to my *perfect match* to be left behind, tossed aside or treated like a child. Whoever this glowering, grumpy, sexy big boss-man was...he would learn that he would not be allowed to boss *me*.

"Do not encourage her, Ronan. I will not have my mate in danger," Kaed replied.

"You'll send me off? I don't even know your names." That was a lie. I was observant, and I listened well. But I made the soft plea anyway, wanting to hear their names spoken just for me. Ronan and Kaed. Kaed and Ronan. Not too weird, for a couple of aliens.

I had no idea what information Warden Egara had sent to him... them about me, but I knew *nothing* about them other than they would be from Prillon Prime, and there would be two of them. That was the sum total of my knowledge.

"I am Commander Makaed Karter of Battlegroup Karter. I am your mate, your primary male." He sighed, looked past me, behind my shoulder. "The Prillon warrior whose lap you are upon is your second, Commander Ronan Wothar."

I turned my head, like in a tennis match, back and forth, relieved to have them confirm that they really were my mates. Two *commanders?* Holy shit. I *really* needed to send Warden Egara a thank you note. They were gorgeous, perhaps a little too intense, but... gorgeous.

"What do you know of me?" I asked.

Commander Karter shook his head. "Nothing."

"Besides the fact you have a birthmark on the right side of your ass and your pussy is bare," Ronan murmured in my ear. "You will call me Ronan."

I squirmed both at the needy way he said the word *pussy*, and at the small command. I loved to push, it was true. But when a strong male pushed back? Damn. My pussy was coated with wet heat. I was in lust.

Kaed—I couldn't think of him as Commander Karter, not when he looked at me like that—took a deep breath and I watched his eyes darken, glancing from where my naked bits were hidden under Ronan's huge shirt, to my eyes, which were most likely broadcasting my desire to claw my way up his chest and ride him. He shuddered and tore his gaze from mine.

"Now is not the time to talk about her pussy, Second. She is in danger. We have to get her out of here. Now." He stood and I had to tilt my head back… and then some more to look at him. He had to be seven feet tall.

"Perhaps we should at least ask her name," Ronan countered.

They both looked to me. "Erica."

Ronan repeated it, as if he'd never heard it before but Kaed's face went from heated to cold. Barren. Ice. There he was…the commander of an alien army.

"Commander Karter," I began.

"I am not your commander," he replied, the scowl on his face genuine and his angular features were hard to read. Maybe, in time, I would figure out their facial expressions.

But for now? Trying to figure out what he was thinking was like staring at a brick wall.

No wonder their females needed the mating collars. A psychic connection would be really handy right about now.

And my mates were both commanders? I had read enough about the Interstellar Coalition Fleet to know that meant they were both really high up the food chain, in charge of an entire sector of space and thousands of people. Kind of like a general back on Earth.

Great. Just great. I wasn't sure how I felt about that. Two

mates were great, but two alien generals? No wonder everything they did seemed so intense.

Ronan stood, lifting me as he did so. He took my hand and gently placed me on my feet. Thank god Ronan was so tall. His shirt came down to my knees, so I felt like I was wearing a heavy cloak. His hand went to my waist to ensure I wouldn't fall. The metal floor of the odd room was cold beneath my bare feet.

"How long until all the injured have been transported to med units?" he asked, turning to a man who stood behind a long table. Similarly dressed to Karter, the warrior's hand flew across the flat panel, as if it were a control board. I looked around, having to peek around Karter's big body to see the rest of them. There were close to two dozen warriors in the room. Some injured. Some obviously medics of some kind.

They'd all seen me naked.

That was just freaking great, too. I didn't flaunt what I had. I was okay with my size. I was big everywhere. Tall. Full ass. Large breasts. Big thighs. A round, soft stomach that was soft as silk to touch. I was not fashionable back home. Too big. Too tall. Too much. I'd worked hard learning to love my body, and my attitude the last couple years had been if you don't like it, move on. I was past the point in my life where I was willing to try to change myself to fit someone else's idea of perfection.

But these warriors made me feel like a tiny Barbie doll.

Maybe they wouldn't mind having a bit more to hold onto.

Two soldiers—the black outfits were now clearly uniforms—carried another warrior up a few steps to a flat area, laid him out and left him. The floor vibrated beneath my feet, and the hairs on my body stood up as if I had the worst case of static electricity. All at once, the body was gone, the vibrations diminished.

"Wow. Can you say, 'Beam me up, Scotty'?"

"Twenty-seven minutes, sir," the man at the controls replied.

I looked around, realized there were injured all around the room. Some were thrashing, moaning, but most were unconscious—or at least I hoped they were that way and not dead. They were being tended to, but there were more wounded than there were medics to help them. A door silently slid open and another injured warrior hobbled in, his arms thrown over the shoulders of two additional Prillon warriors who were helping. He was bigger even than my mates, his face oddly misshapen, like he'd been in the middle of a transformation.

"Fuck. That's Warlord Braun. How the hell did he get on the Varsten? He was sent to the Colony." Karter cursed and Ronan's grip tightened around my hip at the question.

"He volunteered. He's got Hive tech embedded in his brain. We knew you wouldn't be willing to give us Commander Chloe Phan. We were hoping Braun would be able to predict the attack." Ronan's explanation seemed to make the commander even more upset.

"He's got mating fever. Fucking I.C. Never know when to quit, do you?"

Ronan looked away from Karter's accusing stare, and I returned my attention to the gigantic male leaning on two others for help. His uniform was shredded across his abdomen and thighs, blood oozing from his boots every time one of the soles hit the smooth floor.

Warlord Braun was nearly two feet taller then the Prillon duo carrying him. Eight and a half feet tall, at least, his face oddly out of proportion, his jaw too wide. I'd seen a few Atlan warriors guarding the perimeter of the Bride

Processing Center, but they hadn't looked like this. "What's wrong with him?" I asked.

"He's in beast mode," Ronan answered.

Beast mode?

"It's on you if he can't come back." Commander Karter swore and walked away from us, back in operational mode. I could see it now. A general. Someone used to being in charge. And whatever Ronan had done, somehow Karter blamed him for this Warlord's injuries, and his *beast mode.*

"What happened here? Do the medics need help?"

"This ship was attacked by the Hive. About half of those who'd remained on board are dead, but there are survivors. They are being transported to other ships where ReGen pods can save them."

"ReGen pods?"

"Curious, too?" Ronan grinned, but in a flash it was gone. "ReGeneration Podules. They can heal almost any wound, as long as the injured warrior arrives in time."

In time? As in, not dead?

Grins, bare chests, and rippled abs were quickly forgotten. I'd transported into a triage area.

"We have to help," I replied, seeing a guy who was bleeding from his arm. It seemed aliens bled red as well, a pool of it forming at his side. I dashed over, dropped to my knees and pressed the hem of the big shirt I wore against the wound. The person who was helping him looked at me, surprised. He was waving some kind of blue wand over the unconscious fighter.

"Take this, Lady Karter, continue to wave it over his torso."

I frowned, not sure what the device was, or why he was calling me Lady anything, but I did as I was told, continuing to hold pressure. With no medical knowledge beyond what I'd seen on TV, I wanted to be of some help. When the injured man opened his eyes, looked to me, I leaned over him. Smiled. "You're going to be just fine."

"Lady Karter?" he murmured, the question gritted out in obvious pain, but even then, he seemed oddly pleased by his words.

"I'm Erica. You're going to go on a little trip to a med center to get all healed up in one of those pod things." I continued to wave the wand over him and squeezed his arm. "I just got here all the way from Earth. You don't have to be afraid of the transport. If I can do it, you can."

The tension left his face, if even just a little bit. Was he *smiling* at me?

"Twenty-seven minutes?" Karter asked.

"Affirmative, sir."

The vibration and electrical sizzle happened again. I recognized it now as part of transport. Good, another injured warrior was off to get help.

"That's her?"

I turned my head when I heard the new voice. I was the only *her* I could see and knew they were talking about me.

Another huge, caramel colored Prillon stood and stared at me. He, too, had on the black uniform, and he stood next to Commander Karter as if he owned the place.

Must be Karter's mini-me.

Ronan he ignored completely, as if my second were invisible.

Why that bothered me, I couldn't say, but something was going on between my mates, something they had yet to tell me. Unless all Prillon warriors just liked to argue with one another about what to do with a female. But that didn't seem right, either. Not according to that amazing, sexy, perfect matching dream I'd had at the testing center. Those two males had seemed in perfect accord.

"You've been in touch with the Karter?"

"Yes, the shield upgrades have been activated, but we won't know whether or not they'll hold unless the Hive attack."

Commander Karter was staring at me. So was this new Prillon. And Ronan. I seemed to be the center of attention.

"Bard, I don't want my mate blown to bits within ten minutes of transport," Karter snapped.

"Perhaps we will acquire more information from the probe."

"Gods be damned if we don't. We'll lose this fucking war."

"No, we won't." That was Ronan, and he walked around Bard like the new warrior was beneath his notice.

Men.

Ronan continued. "We survived their transport upgrades. Integration Units activating on the battlefield. We've survived worse. We will figure it out. We always do."

"Fight. War. We win." The huge Atlan's voice startled everyone as Warlord Braun was escorted up to the transport pad. His gaze was intense, and he was staring at me. "Fight for mates. Fight. Destroy. Win."

The buzzing sound of the transport pad took the Atlan from us, breaking the spell his relentless stare had cast on me. God, Atlans were intense. Huge. Scary. I would bet this Warlord Braun could rip someone in half with his bare hands. Literally.

The Prillon standing next to Karter—Bard—grinned. When our eyes met, he winked, but remained stern. "Braun is right. So is the I.C. We fight, Commander. We've survived worse."

"My mate has not. She should not be here, on this ship. This is why all non-essential personnel from the Varsten are safely behind the nearest star. We have no idea if they'll strike again without getting the data from that probe. Would you want *your* mate here?"

The other Prillon's shoulders went back as if he'd been insulted. "Of course not."

"The situation is impossible. My mate is in danger, but I am not a simple warrior, Bard. The injured must come first," Karter said, looking to me. "My female suffers, coated in blood, while I am forced to give priority to the wounded." He looked grim. It was obvious he didn't want me here, but did he not want me at all?

"Once they are gone, you will transport with your mate," the other told Karter. "It is only a few minutes. Go back to the Karter. Claim your mate. I will take command here."

Karter narrowed his eyes. "Bard, the Hive will come to Sector 437 next. I do not have the luxury of claiming a mate. Not now."

I was confused. His name was Karter, but wondered why he was talking about himself in the third person. As to the rest? That wasn't confusing at all. He didn't have time for me, didn't want me.

So much for a ninety-nine percent perfect match. But then, that was compatibility, and I could not deny that everything about him made me hot.

"I've sent three of our best warriors out with an I.C. operative to retrieve the probe," the man Karter called Bard replied. "It will take at least twelve hours for them to retrieve it and return. If they have any trouble establishing a visual, it could take longer."

Probe? While I had an NPU, they were speaking in words I didn't understand. What probe? And why a visual? That didn't make sense. Didn't aliens have radar? Or sonar? Something?

When the injured guy before me sucked in a breath, I turned back to him, smiled down. Reassured him the best way I knew how.

Another set of vibrations and static electricity. One more wounded warrior off to receive needed help.

The doors to the transport room slid open again and several additional injured were brought in. Something happened here—although I didn't exactly know where *here* was—some kind of Hive attack. Something bad. Warden Egara told me the Prillon always took mates as a duo in case one of them was killed.

Looking around, that possibility hit home a bit harder than I wanted it to. What if one of these injured warriors was my mate? Was Karter or Ronan?

I didn't even know them yet, but the idea made my gut churn. I'd transported into the middle of a war zone. Warden Egara had warned me about that, but I hadn't really listened. Dead bodies and blood had a way of making everything sink in.

Despite it all, I couldn't step away from the wounded. Somehow, my touch seemed to bring these warriors comfort. The first one had been transported, but there was another I could help, then another. They kept calling me *Lady Karter,* and smiling when I knelt beside them, one warrior's grin wide—despite the fact that he was spitting out blood when he did so.

Were all these Prillon warriors crazy? I was no lady.

I ignored Commander Karter, Commander Wothar and the big one called Bard. I figured out quickly, based on the way everyone was speaking to him, that he was second in command. Even that didn't make sense. If Ronan was a commander, too, why wasn't he in charge of something?

The two males were mine. I knew that. My body definitely knew—and wanted them. Now. But there was so much going on that I didn't understand. I felt like I'd been dropped into a boiling pot of chili, and I was trying to separate the ingredients by hand. Impossible.

So I listened and moved from warrior to warrior, waving the blue wand thing and trying to offer what comfort I could. Which, apparently, was a lot. Their smiles were grim, but every single smile reached the warrior's eyes.

I asked one of them why he was smiling at me. His answer stopped me cold.

"The commander has waited longer than any of us for a mate. You are a gift from the gods, a promise for the rest of us."

A promise, huh? No pressure there.

And as for the commander? My mate? He definitely didn't seem to think I was a gift. A burden maybe.

I caught Ronan watching me and tried to smile, but it felt like a weak attempt, and I knew my eyes were doing a shit job of hiding my disappointment.

This was not a fantasy with a happily-ever-after. This was blood and war. And I'd dropped naked right into the middle of it.

CHAPTER 7

Commander Karter, Battleship Karter, Personal Quarters, One Hour Later

In all my young, foolish imaginings, never had I envisioned this. Nor in my wiser, older years.

Ronan was here, alive, and cradled in his arms as we entered my private quarters was my mate. *Our* mate, half naked and covered in the blood of others, with a smile on her face. Her arms were around his bare neck as he teased her—his mouth close to her ear—about something I could not hear.

That was what a worthy female needed. Teasing. Smiles. A gentle heart and patience from her males.

I was neither gentle nor patient, and the moment I placed the mating collar around both of their necks they would know the chaos of my mind. The heavy ache of responsibility I felt toward every warrior and civilian under my command, my heartache at losing such a close friend in Commander Varsten, the crushing weight of knowing I would always have to choose my people over myself—over her. The burdens I carried lay heavy as death inside me, required a cold, calculated response. That coldness should never touch something so beautiful as my mate.

I had no qualms about taking her body, giving her pleasure, protecting her to the best of my ability. But I would not burden her with the weight I carried, the weight of guilt and sacrifice that command brought. I ordered honorable warriors to their deaths. I made decisions that tore my soul into pieces with no hope nor desire of repair. My burdens would not be hers. My collar would never go around her neck. She was too fragile and soft, too feminine and light to be marred by my darkness.

I was not a soldier or a pilot who could dedicate himself to his mate with no other worry or concern. I was a commander, my first and primary responsibility to protect those who served me. Always. Mate or no mate.

Perhaps she'd learned a hint of it upon her unexpected arrival, transported into the very heart of a disaster. Wounded everywhere. An unplanned way for her to learn the way of things. The order of priorities in my life.

Seeing Erica's beautiful smile, the innocent happiness shining from her eyes, I knew I should walk away and spare her the torment of being mine. But even in that, I failed.

I could not let her go, not now that I'd seen her. So had several fighters in the transport room when she arrived... which flared what I'd considered non-existent protective mating instincts into a raging fire. How dare anyone see her body but her mate and her second? I thought of the claiming ceremony, how it would be witnessed by many, and ground my teeth.

I was torn. I shouldn't keep her, but I wanted no one else to have her. I was too weak to do the right thing, and that fact was like acid in my system, eating me alive from the inside out, making it impossible for me to touch her at all. If I touched her, I'd be lost. Just looking at her was making rational choice impossible.

Perhaps, if I could find the courage and strength to leave now...

"We need to get you cleaned up, female. I do not like seeing my mate covered in blood." Ronan nuzzled her cheek with his nose and walked toward the bathing room as she sighed with contentment and relaxed in his arms.

He seemed to have no issues whatsoever. Perhaps being dead for five years changed one's perspective.

"Okay." Just like that, she agreed. Why wouldn't she? She'd volunteered to be here.

Gods be damned. Soon the sound of water would come on. Then Ronan's uniform shirt she wore would hit the floor and our mate would be naked under the water. Wet. Warm.

She was receptive. I'd seen the look in her eyes upon her arrival. The way her nipples had been pebbled, her cheeks flushed, as if she'd been instantly attracted. She wanted us, approved of our appearance. There had been desire in her eyes when she looked upon me.

I had no business claiming a female when there were so many other worthy warriors who had sacrificed everything to shield our home world and all the worlds under Coalition protection. The list of those who had been tested and waited was long. Why me? Why now?

Ronan and Erica disappeared inside the bathing room, but Ronan did not close the door, his intention clear. I could practically hear him chastising me, *Get your ass in here, idiot. Now!*

Instead, I heard him yell. "Bring that box on the bed when you come in, Kaed."

Box?

Turning slowly, I saw a small, rectangular box sitting atop

61

my bed. With a frown, I walked to inspect it. ATB-Earth was written on the side.

The anal training box that all new Prillon brides received? But an *Earth* bride? And why was the box so small? Normally, the box was several times this large and held a variety of anal plugs in all different sizes. Some brides were not accustomed to taking two lovers when they were first claimed by their Prillon warriors. Our warriors had been using the anal devices to prepare their females for years.

News of my mate's arrival must be all over the Karter, for how else would the ATB have been delivered and waiting for me?

Lifting the lid, I discovered one small, oblong device with odd ribbed joints up and down its length. The joint lines were both vertical and horizontal, forming a grid pattern just above what was obviously a flat handle designed for ease of insertion and removal. The handle was small enough that we could place this in Erica's ass and require her to wear the device to meals or other events and no others would know of our sexual games. Between the gridlines were small, raised bumps.

Odd, but even the idea of placing this inside our mate's round ass made my cock grow to a painful size.

I searched the box for more, found nothing but a small piece of paper of instructions for proper use.

I scanned it quickly. The device was a new model and designed to lubricate the inside of our mate's body. But even better, it was adjustable, the joints movable so the sexual toy would be made longer or wider.

Or both.

We could start small and grow the device to the full size of a Prillon warrior's cock. And no more need to search for lubricant or carry it with us for her comfort.

Better, the plug easily fit in the palm of my hand, a convenient size to carry in a pocket.

The image of pressing Erica between us in a random corridor, a lift, the gardens... Anywhere. We could take her anywhere, anytime. Insert the trainer and fuck her, preparing her for two cocks. When she was ready to handle both of us, we could insert it, prep her with the lube and then both of us could take her together.

I envisioned filling her pussy with my seed—and my child —as Ronan filled her ass, and nearly came in my pants. Gods be damned, I wanted her. Even after knowing her, hell, even knowing I had a mate, for such a short time. When I awoke this morning, I hadn't known of the destruction to Battlegroup Varsten. And I hadn't known I'd have a mate.

Right or wrong, I wanted her pussy around my cock, her cries of pleasure as we claimed her. I wanted her to scream my name as she came and whimper with pleasure as I filled her with my seed. I needed to learn what made her hot. What made her scream.

Fuck.

A commander did not give in to primal urges. Panic. Fear. Lust. Rage. Emotional decisions led to warriors' deaths. Distraction led to destruction. I'd been strong for over a decade. One look at Erica and I was weak, too weak to resist what the Gods had given me. I wanted to spread her wide and taste her sweet pussy, fuck her with my tongue, touch her, everywhere. Mark her with my mouth. I wanted my fucking collar around her neck so no one would dare touch her or harass her in any way. Worse, I wanted my collar around her neck so she could never lie to me, so I would know exactly what she wanted. What she needed. So I could provide. Protect. Seduce. I wanted her to love me. Need me.

And that was where my heart stuttered and I stopped myself cold. The collars, while a sensual pleasure for myself and Ronan, would be hell for her. She'd be with Ronan when he killed, with me when I mourned a warrior's death. She would feel my terror at failing the fleet, the constant fear I buried so deep no one knew it existed. A commander didn't have the luxury of being afraid, and so I buried my rage. My fear. Anything that would endanger my people.

But she would feel it all. Gods help her, it was a curse I wished on no one, let alone my mate, the one female in the universe I was destined to love and protect.

How could I deny destiny? It was as if fate, or the gods themselves, had a hand in her arrival. The fact that Ronan was here, now, alive? Finding him within minutes of discovering I had a mate? Statistically insane. He was a tough bastard. A spy. A liar. A killer.

And if he claimed Erica with me, all of those skills would be used to protect her. I could think of no better second.

And no second with a more disturbing mind. I had no idea where he'd been the last five years, or what he'd done. But I suspected his soul was a black as mine. Erica deserved better than both of us.

"Kaed? I'm not waiting for you!" Ronan's warning fell on deaf ears as I studied the small device in the palm of my hand. I should go in there and insert this in her sexy, round ass. That ass was mine now. Her curves. Her full, heavy breasts. Those lips...

No.

I looked beyond the anal plug to the blood coating my palm. That blood represented the true reality of my life. I groaned in frustration.

I had no right to claim a mate. *We* had no right. Ronan and I were constantly in danger. Fuck, Ronan had pretended to be dead for years. He would have remained so if I hadn't known him. Our jobs were too important to walk away from. I could not abandon my people and make Erica my top priority, as she *deserved* to be. Just like on the transport pad on board Battleship Varsten, the wounded came first. Then the war. Then her.

It was wrong. I was wrong to want a female, a mate. Wrong to bind her to me. Wrong and selfish to claim her. She deserved better than me, than Ronan. She deserved a male who could put her first. Why the *fuck* did the testing program analyze the data otherwise?

"Oh, god. *Yes.*" Erica's voice drifted through the open doorway and broke through my brooding, the sound breathless and needy and full of desire, a voice I'd never heard before but was instantly addicted to.

What was Ronan doing to her?

Was his mouth on her breast?

His tongue in her pussy?

Was he tasting her?

Touching her?

Marking her?

Making her love him?

My clothes hit the ground as I walked, torn from my body. I ripped the fabric, the sound of rending and tearing a fine tribute to my current mood. I gave in, stopped fighting the need building inside me and let the monster free. It was good I wasn't an Atlan, for I now understood what it was to be a beast.

Naked, I entered the room to find Erica clean and wet, pressed with her back to the wall of the cleansing tube. Ronan was on his knees, his mouth on her sweet clit, his fingers pumping in and out of *my* pussy, her hands fisted in his hair. Her eyes were closed, those beautiful, expressive dark blue eyes. Storm clouds. The color was unheard of on Prillon Prime and I found them exotic and beautiful.

"Open your eyes, mate. Look at me as he makes you come." I recognized the command in my voice, was shocked by the sound. I had always imagined I would speak in gentle tones to a female, not this rough, dominating tenor.

For a moment I thought I had scared her, but then her eyes opened and she looked at me, right at me, and I saw no fear there—just raw need. She was not averse to two mates. Two lovers. Doubly demanding and dominant.

Our gazes locked and Ronan applied himself to his task, his fingers moving in and out of her pussy with thick, wet sounds as I watched her eyes grow dark, her cheeks flush, her nipples pebble. But her gaze held, our connection somehow seeming to arouse her more.

Ronan growled, the sound very satisfied just as Erica's body shuddered, every muscle going tight, her large, full breasts swaying with invitation. Her keening cry as she came all over his mouth and fingers made my cock literally pulse and leap toward her, a drop of pre-cum on the tip.

Her cum. Her seed. Her male. I was hers now. Gods help her.

Without asking, I moved to Ronan, who was still on his knees. Yanking him to his feet, I shoved him behind me and out of the shower tube. I stepped within and faced our mate. He protested, so I held out the anal plug and instructions for him. He took them and I stepped under the water, quickly washing. Watching Erica from Earth the entire time. I would not touch something so beautiful and precious with blood on my hands.

"Gods bless us, Kaed. Did you read this?" Ronan asked from behind me. I could hear him stripping, hear the eagerness in his voice. He'd entered the tube with his uniform on, probably so focused on our mate's needs he didn't take the time to strip.

"Yes." I did not take my eyes from Erica's. I had yet to touch her, the need building in me like a bomb about to explode. Clean now, I gave her my full attention. "Do you want this, Erica? Want me? Want us? Because if I touch you, there is no going back."

She lifted her chin, the top of her head not even reaching my shoulder. Her size was larger than Chloe, another from Earth. Every part of her was bigger. Big hips, big breasts, big ass. More for me to grab, to grip, to suck. Lick. Fuck. Her gaze was not just full of desire, but challenge. "Yes. I know what I want. I'm not a child, Commander."

"Kaed." I didn't want her to call me commander. I was not her commander. Or Karter. With her, like this, I was a warrior, a male, and nothing more. "I know I told you Karter earlier, but my mind was in battle mode. I would prefer you call me Kaed, my first name."

"Kaed." The sound of my name on her lips made me shudder; still I did not touch her, allowing the anticipation to bubble through my veins like the strongest drug.

"I am your primary male, Erica." I tipped my head out of the tube. "Ronan is your second. Do you understand what that means?" I had to know that she understood what was about to happen. Ronan was, perhaps, even more stubborn than I. If we claimed her, neither of us would be gentle with our words. We were hard, inside and out.

Her skin turned an adorable shade of pink that I had seen only a handful of times before on the other human females I knew. It crept from her cheeks, down her neck and all the way to the hard tips of her breasts. Was our curvy mate feeling embarrassment? Desire? Perhaps both?

"Warden Egara explained it to me. I knew... I knew there would be two of you." The last three words came out with a wobble in her breath, as if she was having trouble getting air into her lungs. As if she were pleased with the idea.

Good. So was I.

"Gods be damned, Kaed. Get on with it!" Ronan growled

from behind me, but I had him blocked. There was no way for him to reach Erica without my permission.

"I will not rush this, Ronan," I growled.

"She is aroused and primed. I have her taste on my tongue. I could have given her three more orgasms by now. If you don't want her, get out of my way."

"*She is mine.*"

"And mine. Or have you forgotten that?"

I frowned, watching as the mindless lust faded from Erica's eyes. The impertinence of her words annoyed me even more. "Do you two need to get a room? I can come back later." I frowned. A room? We were in a room.

"No."

"No."

We spoke as one. In this, Ronan and I were in perfect agreement. I didn't want her going anywhere.

She tipped up her pert chin. "Well, I want both of you. Inside me. I want to come until I can't remember my own name. I want the mating collar around my neck, so I know what you're both feeling, like I had in my testing dream, and I want it all right fucking now, gentlemen. So, are we going to do this, or should I find the cafeteria, or wherever you all get your food, and grab a snack while you act like cavemen, beating your chests, trying to figure out who's in charge?"

CHAPTER 8

Erica

The Commander—Kaed—grinned. A slow, lethal smile that made him look even sexier. Dark. Dangerous. Hot as hell. And he stood up to me. He didn't seem to wilt under my bold nature.

"What did you say to me, mate?"

Oh, shit. I'd gone too far that time. The commander, Kaed, my *primary* male, the one who was supposed to be ninety-nine percent *perfect* for me, glared at me like I'd just threatened to take down his entire battleship. Or worse. His gaze was hot, intent and focused. He looked all too eager to answer my challenge.

And my pussy wept.

Not the first time the disconnect between my brain and my mouth had gotten me in trouble. I tended to say what I thought, without a filter. Which, so far, hadn't been working out all that well. Especially with Earth men.

But these two were *not* human. God no. They were huge.

Ronan was golden all over, every inch of him like a gilded god. And Kaed? He was tall, dark and dangerous. Dark caramel skin, dark hair and eyes. They both had the angular features of the Prillon race, not human looking, but humanoid and exotic. Intense. Probably seven feet tall, making me feel tiny despite my five-foot-nine inches, size eleven shoes and enough curves for two women. And then there was the non-stop, never-ending muscles. Chest muscles. Thighs. Back muscles. God, even their necks were lined with power.

And they were *naked.*

I glanced down.

Oh, yeah. And huge—*huge*—cocks.

I was about to cream myself just staring at Kaed's cock. I wanted it inside me. Now. Stretching me open as Ronan positioned himself at my ass. I'd never done any kind of ass play before, never even considered it. Why would I if I had a hard time finding a guy who knew what to do with my pussy, let alone my ass.

But that was before the testing dream. It had been like an epiphany, a porno that had somehow told me what I really wanted. What I really needed. That dream came back full-force, my body more than willing to experience the bliss I'd felt in the testing, taking two cocks. Add that to Ronan's magical mouth... god, I'd come within a minute. From oral. Fingers, too, but O.M.G.

I was ready to give them *everything,* all of me, just like in the bride processing dream. But all Kaed seemed to want to do was *talk* to me and *argue* with Ronan. With his cock all hard and pointing straight at me.

God.

Men.

Whatever. I was tired. I'd transported halfway across the galaxy—well, really, really far. I actually had no idea where I was in comparison to Earth. So, I'd gone through all the testing, transported—excited to arrive and be claimed by two sexy hunks who instantly adored me. Instead? Well, I'd spent all of last night—my last night on Earth and in my bed—in fitful sleep wondering if I was about to make the biggest mistake of my life, then gone through about a million questions at the Brides Center, hours of physical and mental testing, the dream sex, transported across the freaking universe, arrived in the middle of a medical emergency after what looked like a nasty battle—which kind of freaked me out—and for what?

For these jerks to fight over me like they were hungry wolves and I was just a piece of meat? The alpha wolf didn't really want me, but he didn't want to let Ronan have me either.

My *primary* mate hadn't even really touched me yet. I didn't count his carrying me from the transport platform. That had been duty... not desire. Not once had I felt his touch as a caress. Not one kiss. Nothing. No compliments. No smiles. Nothing. He'd scowled, complained about my presence, made it known he was not happy that I was in danger. But nothing intimate. Personal. He'd barely spoken to me at all.

Pathetic. And disappointing. Very, very disappointing.

My eyes burned. My throat closed up.

Tears? Damn it. I was even more tired than I thought.

"Look. Forget it. Get out of my way." I shoved at the commander's chest—I couldn't call him Kaed right now, not when he was being so distant—and tried to step past him.

"No." His hand wrapped around my waist, the touch electrifying. His arm was hard as a rock, not letting me pass but not trapping me either. The arm was more like a command to stay right where I was, an extension of his will.

Enough. I was too far past exhausted to care what came

out of my mouth, and too frustrated with my needy body to try to maintain control. The testing dream had been so amazing. It was probably stupid to think that the three of us would all be so content and connected and happily-ever-after instantly. But this weird tension between my mates? I didn't understand it. If they didn't want to share a mate with one another, then why had the commander chosen Ronan to be his second? And if the commander didn't want a mate at all, why did he go through the testing? He had to be in their system for me to be matched to him. Right?

"Maybe the matching program made a mistake." My sigh was deep, and it hurt, crushing my chest as the air left my lungs. Not only did he not appear to want a mate—other than the erection, which could be written off as purely biological—he hadn't been attentive or comforting or caring. At. All. Completely naked, I had transported into a mess, blood and wounded warriors—I'd held my own, kept my cool—and he'd acted like he didn't want me around. Not then. Not now, when he had a curvy, naked woman in his shower.

Aroused, willing woman shows up, begging him to claim her, and what?

I thought I'd be riding his cock with my back against the wall, screaming his name by now. That's what I'd really, really wanted to be doing. Not this. Not holding back tears and wondering if I'd made the biggest, most colossal, mistake of my life. The walk of shame back to Earth was pretty fucking far.

His dark eyes were like pools of black. I had no idea what he was thinking, or feeling, or wanting as he stared at me, every muscle in his body so tight he was like a bowstring about to snap.

"Perhaps."

"What?" Ronan spoke the word for me. What the fuck kind of game was this guy playing?

Karter stepped forward, and I moved back as he advanced until my ass hit the smooth, wet wall. My hands lifted instinctively to his chest, to hold him off—or so I thought—but I didn't push him away. I *stroked* the heated skin beneath my palms. The Prillons were warm to the touch, like a human with a high fever. So hot. Hard, like their muscles were made of granite.

"I want you, female. I want to lift you off your feet and bury my cock in your tight pussy. I want to fuck you and fill you with my seed."

Oh? Was that all?

"About time." I lifted my hand, traced his full lips with my fingertip. He and Ronan were both so big... thank god. I loved that I seemed almost small with them. "Are you always this stubborn?" I asked.

"Yes," Ronan answered.

I stared up at Karter—Kaed, I could think of him as Kaed now that he was mine again—and tilted my head back. "Kiss me, Kaed. Kiss me and lift me up. I've wanted it... needed it, even on Earth. Fuck me against the wall like you want to. Do it." I was ready, still wet and needy from Ronan's attention, and Kaed's gorgeous body, and the anticipation of what I hoped was about to happen. I wanted what he was offering me. Hot sex. Two devoted males. His seed. A baby. I'd wanted to be a mother for as long as I could remember. I wanted everything.

He moved as if I had unleashed a caged, wild animal. His mouth crashed down on mine as he lifted me off my feet. With a gasp, I wrapped my legs around his waist, opening myself in invitation. His tongue slid into my mouth and his cock deep in my pussy in one powerful thrust.

My head angled back and I closed my eyes.

"Yes," I moaned, when he lifted his head so we could breathe. Sooooo yes. Warden Egara wasn't just getting a thank you note, but balloons and maybe a big-ass teddy bear.

The sounds coming from my throat were primal, and I made no attempt to stop them or hide my pleasure from this warrior. I'd told him what I wanted. Offered my naked body to him. Hell, I transported across a galaxy for him. He was mine now. I felt it in the tense lines of his shoulders, in the nearly mindless thrusting of his hips as he fucked me with his huge cock. Fast. Deep. Hard.

I'd been aroused and ready for Ronan, coming easily for him. What woman wouldn't come from his prowess with his tongue and fingers. He'd found my clit and G-spot without a road map and a flashlight.

Since I was all sensitive and warmed up, just a thick cock stretching me open, stroking over places deep inside had me coming so easily. Perhaps it was because my mind wasn't stopping me. I wasn't inhibited. I wasn't shy. I wasn't even thinking about whether I'd shaved today. My brain was focused solely and completely on how good he made me feel. And I wasn't even wearing the collars I'd seen in the testing dream.

I came with a sharp cry that only seemed to encourage him to increase his pace until I was gasping for air, unable to breathe, unwilling to stop. Until I screamed as another orgasm ripped through my entire body like an earthquake, shaking every muscle, every bone.

His seed spilled deep inside me, a hot stream that I hoped would find its way deeper, giving me the child I wanted. Literally met the guy a few hours ago and now I wanted his kid. But, the testing program knew what I needed and it gave me Kaed, so I wasn't delaying. At all.

When it was over, he shuddered and pulled his still hard cock free. I stared down at it—he was ready to go again...

already?—as he gently washed the remnants of his seed from my pussy and thighs. I wondered at the odd behavior.

"You ready to share now, Commander?" Ronan asked.

Kaed actually turned his head to growl over his shoulder at his second. "Share? You tasted her first. I will not forget that."

Ronan remained silent as Kaed rinsed and dried me with a warrior's efficiency, his touch gentle but not sensual in any way. He wouldn't even look me in the eyes. When he was done, he lifted me and carried me—no strain on his part—into the main quarters where a living room area was set up, complete with two large sofas, a small table with four chairs made for someone much taller than I was—my feet would dangle and swing like I was a three-year-old if I tried to sit there—and a bed more than big enough for the three of us.

I thought Kaed would go for the bed, but he carried me to the sofa instead and sat down with me on his lap.

"Now, mate, you will attend to Ronan."

"Yes." I was relaxed and pliant in his arms, the three orgasms they'd given me making my body feel like a pool of melted caramel. But my pussy was swollen and wet, and even though he'd cleaned me, cum still slipped from me. My breasts were heavy, my nipples tight peaks. My blood still pounded and my clit throbbed. I was tired, but I wanted this to be right. I wanted to make sure both of my mates knew they were gorgeous and perfect and *wanted*. "I want you, Ronan. I want both of you."

Ronan had followed behind, the slim device in his hand as he stood next to where we sat. His cock was at eye level, bulging and full. Huge, like Kaed's. Now that I knew what it felt like to have Kaed inside me, I wanted to feel that again. I wanted to know what it felt like to have each of them inside me. I needed to claim them both. To give them both pleasure. If I were carrying their child, I did not want to know whose seed had taken hold. I wanted the baby to be *ours*. All three of ours. Equally. If there was some kind of DNA testing to determine who the father was, I didn't want it. We were a family now. They were my family. They were mine.

I was all in on this. When I walked into the Brides Testing center in Florida, I'd been absolutely positive about what I wanted. I had no doubts then, I still didn't now.

And if these two were truly mine, forever, as Warden Egara had promised me, I was going to get my way, at least about something as vitally important to our future as this.

Not waiting for instructions or demands I would have to ignore, I leaned forward and took Ronan's cock in my hand, guiding it to my mouth. He staggered forward, his groans growing in volume as his pre-cum coated my tongue and his cock jerked in my hold.

"Ah, mate," he said, then clenched his jaw.

He was big, too big for me to take in fully, but I worked his tip between my lips, swirling my tongue around the thick head as if he were my favorite flavor of ice cream cone. I worked his base with my hand, gently leading him where I wanted him to go as I played.

When I had him with his knees on the floor, I broke free and turned in Kaed's arms with my ass up, presenting my wet, dripping pussy to Ronan.

Both warriors froze as if in shock.

"What are you doing, female?" Kaed asked.

"Erica?" Ronan spoke at nearly the same instant, with his gaze squarely on my upturned ass. I knew he could see my pussy lips from this angle, and probably some of Kaed's seed slipping from me.

I smiled up at Kaed as I wrapped my hand around the base of his cock. "What? Can't I please both of you at once?"

His quickly indrawn breath prevented him from speaking as I lowered my head and swallowed as much of his hard length as I could. He felt different, tasted different than Ronan, against my tongue. Behind me, Ronan cursed, his fingers pushing forward into my pussy.

"She's so fucking wet, Kaed." His voice was filled with wonder. "She's coated in your seed."

Kaed didn't speak but buried his hands in my hair with a soft moan as I worked him with my lips and tongue. I shifted my hips, working myself on Ronan's fingers.

"This is going to feel good, mate. I promise you." Ronan spoke, but I did my best to ignore him, focused on the task at hand until the hard, rounded tip of something cold pressed against me...*there*.

I lifted my head and gasped. Was he sliding something into my...

With a soft pop, something entered my bottom, the handle sliding to a stop pressed to my ass cheeks. I'd been too focused on Kaed's cock to resist the entry and the object slid in with a smooth glide, as if Ronan had filled me with lube, but I knew there had been none. It would have been cold and slippery, but I'd felt nothing. "Ronan? What?"

He leaned over my back, his large hands splayed over my ass as he kissed the length of my spine, his body heat like a hot blanket. "Hush, mate. This is how we will prepare you to take both of us. One in your pussy, one in your ass. We have to prepare you because you are tight. Too tight. But I promise you nothing but pleasure. Trust me."

So far, the object felt strange, but good. Nerve endings I didn't even know existed were awakened, the sensations different, yet incredible. The slight increase in pressure made my pussy even more eager to be filled. I wondered what his cock would feel like pressed deep inside me against *that*.

I didn't want to wait. Reaching back, I grabbed his cock, positioned at my entrance and shoved back, taking him inside me. Claiming him.

"Erica, no!" He leaned back, sitting up on his haunches immediately, but I had him deep, pressed against whatever toy he'd just put in my ass, and I wasn't letting him go. I arched up and back, locked my hands around his neck and held on for dear life, his cock deep.

On Earth, I'd be considered a slut going after two guys like this. Practically strangers and not just basic Tab A into Slot B sex here. There were toys and two guys and me, my inner sex goddess coming out to play. I liked her. *A lot.*

"Yes. I want you inside me." I pressed down, angling my hips to take him deeper, squeezed my inner muscles. Let go. Over and over until I was on the brink of another orgasm. He was as big as Kaed, not as thick in girth, but a touch longer. He bottomed out and it pushed me just shy of painful.

"Fuck. I'm sorry, Kaed." Ronan's cock jumped inside me, and I knew he was holding back. Why would he not grab hold and fuck hard?

Why? His response was odd, and a bit disturbing. Why was he apologizing for fucking me? Why weren't his hands on my breasts? His mouth on my neck? Why wasn't he urging me on? Telling me he wanted me? Couldn't wait to fill me with his seed? Why was I the only one into it right now?

Confused, I looked to Kaed for answers, found him staring at my bouncing breasts. "Kaed?"

He tore his gaze from my body and glanced at me, then Ronan. "She does not know our ways, Ronan."

Sex was sex, not matter what planet you were on. Right?

"But I do. I won't come. I won't give her my seed." Ronan's hands trembled on my hips as he attempted to push me off his lap. I stayed put.

"What's the matter? Don't you want me?"

Behind me, Ronan groaned at my question. He was panting but Kaed stared at me like he was analyzing a puzzle, a puzzle he desperately needed to solve.

Kaed's stare was making my pussy clench, making me hot. I was about to come again because until now, I'd never been watched before.

God, my mate had dangerous eyes.

Ronan's fingers dug into my hips, just enough that I knew he was fighting himself, fighting his need to come inside me. "The primary male has first rights to a child, mate," he bit out. "I am not allowed to fuck you in your pussy, to give you my seed, until you are carrying Kaed's child."

"Are you serious?" That was stupid. I told them as much. "Aren't you both mine? I don't want to look at my child and think—*Oh, that's Kaed's baby*—and *Oh, that one is Ronan's*. I don't want that. Are we a family or not?"

Why were we having this conversation now? *Now*, with Ronan's cock inside me and Kaed's eyes focused on my breasts, the taste of his cock still thick on my lips?

Ronan held perfectly still, waiting for Kaed's answer as much as I. We were both at Kaed's mercy, it seemed, unless I wanted to walk away from these mates and chose another primary male. But even then, according to Warden Egara, I would have to wait thirty days. That might break my heart. I'd only been here a few hours, and I already wanted to keep them. Both of them.

And Kaed had come inside me. His seed made Ronan's passage easier. I could get pregnant from this first time. Warden Egara had offered me birth control, but I didn't want it. I was pushing thirty and I was ready. She said it was up to me, that Prillon males never said no to a child. Ever.

Seemed that was wrong, too. They shared my body, but I had to take turns making babies with them? That felt wrong. I didn't want to live like that. Maybe if I had three dark-haired little ones in a row, I'd take some time and try to go for gold, but right now, I didn't want to think like that.

"You're both commanders, you make the rules," I practically shouted at them.

"We are a family," Kaed said, finally. "Give our mate what she wants, Ronan. Fuck her. Fill her with your seed. Our child will be loved and protected regardless of whose seed takes root."

I couldn't stop my smile, or the jiggle of my hips as I teased Ronan closer to orgasm. This was huge. I wasn't sure how or why they had this custom, but I felt the significance of Kaed's concession, even if I didn't fully understand it. Why shouldn't Ronan enjoy this same pleasure? Why was there a value difference between the two of them?

"Thank you, mate," I replied. "You just made me very happy." And if I'd had the collar I was promised around my neck, he would know that.

Maybe they had to order them? Or wait? Maybe they had to claim me first? Fuck me? Make sure we were compatible? I didn't know, and this wasn't the time to ask, because we'd been talking waaaaayyy too much with Ronan's cock deep inside me and Kaed's thick cock so close to my lips.

Leaning forward so Ronan could fuck me harder, I moved myself deeper into Kaed's lap, took his cock in one hand and his heavy balls in the other. "Now I will make both of you very happy, *mates*."

Ronan fucked me then, hard and fast and deep, his driving thrusts moving my mouth over Kaed's cock as he took me. The slap of flesh on flesh filled the room. Groans intermingled with gasps.

"Touch her clit, Ronan," Kaed ordered. "Make her scream around my cock."

Mouth full of thick, hot cock, I could only moan and writhe as Ronan's hand slipped around my ass to my hip. Lower.

Then he was fingering my clit as he moved, driving me to

distraction. The object in my bottom only added to all the sensations bombarding me.

My scream was muffled by Kaed's hard length, but he must have felt it as Ronan pushed me over the edge. Hot, wet cum filled my pussy and my mouth, filling me, marking me. I knew that's how these alpha males liked to think of it. I was very much theirs now.

But to me it was the opposite. *They* were mine. That cum was mine. Their cocks were mine. They gave me their seed, their essence, but held back the deepest darkest parts of their minds. They didn't give me their collars, or their hearts. And that was totally unacceptable when I was willing to give them everything.

But I had time. Eventually, my stubborn warriors would give me what I wanted. A collar. Our connection. A real mating.

They were mine, even if they didn't know exactly what that meant.

They would learn not to mess with an Earth girl.

CHAPTER 9

Erica, Personal Quarters, Battleship Karter

I stared out the window at all the stars. There was nothing to see but blackness and... the entire universe. The lights in the room were dimmed, set by either Kaed or Ronan before they left. I vaguely remember being kissed on the shoulder and told to sleep, that they needed to go to the command deck.

I had no idea what that meant, and at the time, had been too tired to care. They could be belly dancers and I wouldn't have minded. Maybe it was the amazeballs sex or the road-trip across the galaxy, but I barely remembered what happened after coming all over Ronan's cock with the taste of Kaed's seed on my tongue.

Sex had never been that good... or that disappointing. I bit my lip, the sting meant to drive back the stupid, worthless tears forming in my eyes. The sex? Awesome. Unreal. Completely off the charts. Out of this world. *Ha!* But our *mating?* I wasn't so sure about that. I still remembered the way Kaed had looked at me in the shower, how he'd conveniently forgotten to give me his collar, despite the fact that I'd told him—told them both—that I wanted the connection, that closeness. I wanted them to claim me.

Maybe I was too tired to think straight. I remembered that they'd wrapped themselves around me in bed, made me feel safe and warm and completely protected. I'd never felt so exhausted or content in my life.

I'd slept and slept hard.

And when I woke up? Space. Beautiful. Magnificent. Brilliant. No light pollution or haze. Just me staring out this window at the stars.

For the first time in my life, after countless hours looking up, I finally felt like the stars were staring back.

Because outside this window was space, there was no night or day. I had no idea what time it was or how long I had slept. I didn't care. None of it mattered. I had two mates who craved me as much as I craved them. Oh, they were a little resistant, it seemed, but still... orgasms made me see rainbows and unicorns in my mind.

I was happy, right? Two mates. Lots of crazy sex. And out the window?

Everything my little stargazer's heart could ever dream of. I searched for familiar constellations, Earth's moon, anything to give me my bearings, but it all looked as if someone had taken the stars and thrown them into a blender. Nothing made sense. There were no patterns I recognized. Nothing familiar. No constellations I knew. Just points of light, some big, some small. The planets in this star system were so close I could see the nearest one, and it was three times larger than Earth's moon. And red, not silver. A fleet of smaller ships of all different types and sizes floated in and out of view, moving through the emptiness of space just outside the window. It was like watching a live action sci-fi movie through my window.

I really was in an episode of *Star Trek*, but I wasn't the red shirt ensign who always got killed off. Not in this movie. I was the heroine. The movie star who got to fall in love with the commanders of the fleet and wear their wedding band—or collar—same thing here—around my neck.

Except I didn't, and I had no idea why.

I stood wrapped in just the chocolate-colored sheet I'd pulled from the bed, since I couldn't find any closets or any kind of clothes. I wasn't sure if they planned to keep me naked for a while or not. The idea had some good points, but my big boobs needed a bra.

"Hello!"

I turned at the sound of a woman's voice. The door had opened and closed behind her without making any noise. "There you are! Erica, right? Did you get a good rest?"

The woman was small, tiny compared to me. She looked like she was part Asian, with light cream-colored skin and straight, jet-black hair, but her accent was pure American and she was speaking English. Someone from home!

I smiled. I couldn't help it. First real day and I'd already met someone from home. It helped, made me happier than I'd thought it would. I didn't feel so alone. At least that was the case, until I saw the golden collar around her neck.

So, she was a Prillon mate. Like me.

Except her males had claimed her, made it official.

She was staring, her smile fading a bit, the brightness in her eyes fading to concern.

"I slept like the dead."

Her smile said she understood, but her black uniform surprised me. She was dressed like the warriors I'd seen. She even had some kind of space gun strapped to her hip. A mate and a warrior? Did they allow that? Not that I wanted to fight, but my mates had made me think no female was ever allowed to be in danger out here.

This Earth woman proved that to be a lie. A big, fat excuse not to give me what I had been promised. Why would the commander not put his collars on us and make us a family? What was he trying to hide?

"I'm Erica. Erica Roberts." I held out my hand. She pushed it aside and came in for a hug, a bear hug. Guess she was excited to see someone from home, too.

"I'm Chloe and I came from Earth. I'm so excited to have another woman here, one who knows what a cheeseburger is and what green grass looks like." She was warm and friendly and I immediately liked her. I felt relief, surprisingly, with her sharing my same customs and upbringing. I wasn't alone in my past out here. Someone would understand me.

"I'm also thrilled that Karter was matched. He tested a long time ago and I think he forgot all about it."

"He's a busy guy," I said.

She nodded. "Definitely a workaholic. As for your second, I've never met him before, even though he's in the I.C. with me. Strange." She thought for a moment, then shook it off.

I had no idea what the I.C. was, but it sounded like they both had the same kind of job. "What's the I.C.?"

Her eyes grew round, but she tilted her head, as if judging me, then shrugged. "You're matched to Karter, so you must be a badass."

A badass? "Not really."

Her smile was patient, as if she knew I was lying to her. I wasn't. "Whatever. You're his, and Commander Wothar's, so there's no reason not to tell you the truth. The I.C. is the Coalition Fleet's Intelligence Core, kind of like the CIA in outer space. I joined a few years ago, when I volunteered to serve in the fleet. I'm Commander Chloe Phan, at your service." She bowed at the waist with a grace and flare that said she knew how to move, and probably how to fight.

"So, Ronan is in the alien CIA?"

"Yes. Doing shit so secret even I don't know about it. He had something to do with the Varsten being wiped out. That's why Karter's so pissed off at him. That and they were friends from way back. Ronan has been off the grid for about five years. Everyone thought he was dead."

"Even Kaed?" I asked, stunned.

"Kaed? Who's that?" Her nose scrunched up in an adorable way that I envied. She was everything I was not— petite, thin, a fighter.

"Commander Karter."

She chuckled. "Name's Kaed, huh? That's news I can sell for some extra tech in requisitions."

"No. Makaed Karter. But Ronan calls him Kaed."

"And you?" Chloe saw too much. Either that or she heard the hurt in my voice. But then, she was an outer space spy, trained to notice everything. "What do you call him?"

"I don't know yet." Staring at her collar was making me wonder if I'd made a mistake coming out here after all. Who knew I'd have collar envy? Yes, it was a pretty gold color against her perfect, light brown skin, but still. Collar envy? That was just weird.

Thank god she changed the subject, joining me to stare out the window. "What did you do, back on Earth?"

"I have a master's degree in astronomy."

"Awesome. A science geek."

"Totally." I laughed. "Didn't expect to ever hear that term again." I looked down at her. She had a calm manner that put me at ease. "What did you do?"

"Military first. Then I served in the Coalition Fleet. They sent me home—long story involving a self-serving asshole who set me up—"

"I hate them," I said.

"Me, too. But I got the last laugh. Was a 9-1-1 operator for a while, back on Earth, then volunteered as a bride. Soon as I got here, Commander Karter looked up my fleet record and I was right back in the mix where I wanted to be."

"And your mates? They're okay with you being in danger all the time?" I needed to know, because that was the exact opposite of a ton of words Ronan and Kaed had said to me.

"No. But I outrank both of them, so they couldn't order me not to fight. It was 'take me as I am', or choose someone else."

Damn, I wish I were half as confident as she appeared to be.

"Nice collar," I offered. The proof of their choice—and acceptance of their female—was solidly around her neck.

Her hand drifted to the golden collar, her fingers running over it almost absently. "Thanks." She sighed and we stood in silence for a few minutes, each lost in our own thoughts. "The view is amazing, isn't it?" she asked.

"It's beautiful. I don't recognize anything you'd see on Earth, but I've been making up my own constellations."

"Of course you'd be into stars."

"I worked at an observatory for a few years doing research on the Supergiants, especially Sirius. We think it's over two hundred billion years old. Part of the reason I wanted to be a bride was to see if I could access the Coalition's star charts and astrological data."

"They'll have a lot of that. They're all over the galaxy and have been for centuries."

"That's what I was hoping." My smile was sheepish. Yes, I wanted amazing mates and babies and a happily ever after, but I wanted more than that. I needed knowledge like I needed water, but I couldn't explain all that in the first five minutes. Probably scare her off, and she was the first human I'd met out here. "Stars are kind of my thing."

"So where are you on the Big Bang?" she turned and looked up at me.

Loaded question. "Undecided."

She laughed. "That sounds like a really cool job. You must be ridiculously smart. Math makes my head hurt."

I shrugged because test scores and college rank didn't really matter out here. I pointed. "See those five stars in a row. They're vertical?"

"Yes." Her chin was tipped up and she was following where I aimed my finger. "Then it turns to the right, then back up."

"Like a box!"

"I see it as a gift box. The cluster at the top is like a curly bow."

"I see it! Constellation Gift Box."

"Sure." Not exactly what I had in mind for a name, but at least she was seeing what I did.

"Well, Earth girl, you've seen out into space, had your body rocked by your mates and caught up on your beauty sleep. So how about a tour around the ship? I mean, you're Lady Karter now, in charge of the entire civilian side of things, so I'd think you'd want to see the inside of the battleship you run now. And it's named after your mate's family."

Battleship Karter. Suddenly, all those third person references made more sense. Kaed hadn't been talking about himself, but about the ship with the same name we were on.

"Wait. Did you just say I'm in charge of something?"

My disbelief must have been clear on my face, because Chloe laughed. "Oh, yeah. You're the boss now. Anything not military will have to go through you. School. Food. Social events. Civil disagreements."

Holy hell, this was in introvert's worst nightmare. "Like what?"

"Not a lot happens around here to argue about, but let's say two people are bickering over personal quarters, or someone is playing their music too loud."

"Are you kidding me?"

She shook her head. "Nope. As the commander's mate, you're like the mayor of the battlegroup. The only person who outranks you is Karter himself, and only because he's the military commander. You're like the civilian commander. He only outranks you because we live in a war zone, but most civilian or not-critical decisions will be yours to make."

Not a big deal, right? I could breathe through this. "How many people live in my little space town?"

"Just over five thousand. But with the incoming survivors from the Varsten, it's more like nine thousand at the moment." Chloe's grin was absolutely unrepentant. She was enjoying this. "Don't worry. I'm sure you'll do great. You're brilliant, so you'll adapt."

So much for having someone from home who would understand me. She was just as crazy as the rest of them appeared to be. "I don't know anything about any of that. I'm a total introvert, Chloe. I'm serious. I'm more comfortable with a calculator or a telescope than people. And stars don't talk back. They don't change."

"Won't matter. The people on this ship will come and ask you anyway. And you have a lot of personnel around to help you." She punched me on the shoulder and I was proud of myself for not flinching. "Come on. Let's get out of here so you can meet your devoted fans. Everyone wants to meet you. You're a celebrity."

A celebrity? Was she insane? Only one way to find out. I was *Lady Karter* now, mayor of a space town in a war zone with nine-thousand aliens depending on me for answers.

Holy shit. Warden Egara hadn't told me a damn thing about this. But I was not a coward. Just because I didn't *like* to be around people didn't mean I couldn't do it when I had to. And no way I was going to hide in this room for the rest of my life. "Okay. I'd love to look around. And I'm starving."

"I'm an I.C. Commander. I think I can handle a tour and lunch."

"Lunch? How long was I out?"

She checked something on her wrist, some kind of data display built into the arm of her uniform. "Looks like you transported back to the Karter about sixteen hours ago, give or take." She tapped something and shrugged. I noticed she did that a lot. Nothing seemed to bother her. "They run on a twenty-five-hour day out here, so it's not a bad adjustment. Really similar to what your body is already used to. You'll adapt in no time."

"I never sleep that long." But it did explain why I was so hungry. I hadn't had a real meal since before the processing dream on Earth. And then... well, Kaed and Ronan had worn me out.

I knew I blushed as the thought crossed my mind, but Chloe just laughed. "I bet you were busy. Post-battle adrenaline plus new mates. Wow, must have been explosive."

I didn't respond because I had a feeling she wasn't digging for dirty details, just stating fact.

"I'll start at the beginning then. Karter asked me to come and check on you since you were zonked out. I can't believe you transported *twice* and still were conscious enough for sexy times."

I had no idea the effects transporting had on other women from Earth, so I didn't think anything special about my supposed accomplishment. But I didn't have time to explain any of that, because Chloe kept talking.

"Karter is in charge of this ship, like I said, so he's got

work. Non-stop, especially after what happened on the Varsten. Ronan, too. They'll be back, I promise. They're tracking down the data on that probe. In the meantime, we'll go on that tour and I'll give you a Welcome to Space 101 class."

That sounded great.

"Can we start with clothes?" I asked.

Chloe laughed. "Ah yes, that is a class all in itself." She walked into the bedroom and to a wall unit that looked like polished black marble, until bright green lines appeared, making a kind of grid. "This is the S-Gen machine. That stands for Spontaneous Matter Generator. It's like an old-fashioned 3-D printer on Earth with a major upgrade. It will make you new clothes every day. When you're done, you dump them in the ship's recycling system."

"You throw away your clothes?"

"Recycle them. And yes. We do. It's really handy and you never have to do laundry."

Sweet. I followed her in and watched as she fiddled with the machine.

"I wonder if your measurements are in here from the transport data." She wasn't talking to me, but herself. By her grunt of satisfaction, I assumed she found what she was looking for. "Karter's family color? Brown? Sweet." She eyed me as if deciding what kind of clothing I might want to wear. "That will look totally awesome with your hair, just like that sheet."

What?

"Duh, the sheet is brown. The couch is brown. Should have known." She fiddled some more, then her shoulders fell and her grin faded. "Okay, Lady Karter, I set this machine to your specs. It knows it belongs to you now. So, what do you want to wear? Military spec uniform, like me? You can space walk and take a few hits from an ion blaster without getting hurt. Or you can go for the traditional dress worn by most of the Prillon mates I've seen. They are pretty, fall to your feet, and remind me of something a Roman goddess would wear."

Ion blasters did not sound like something I wanted to deal with. And, I was trying to seduce my mate into giving me his damn collar, so we'd go with the dress. "Let's go goddess."

"Excellent." She raised her brows again. "Want a little support for the girls?"

"Definitely." Glad she'd thought to ask, I stared in wonder as the black panel lit up with some green lines, and the next thing I knew a custom-made dress and soft ankle boots had transported directly into my bedroom. The dress was soft, a gorgeous shade of brown, like my favorite milk chocolate bar, the fabric thicker than I'd imagined it would be, with built in support for my large breasts.

She left me to shower and squirm into the clothing. I didn't have make-up or anything to mess with, so it didn't take me long. But there was *one* thing that made me a bit... uncomfortable. "It's a bit breezy under this dress."

Chloe laughed. "I can make you underwear, if you want, but one look at your curves in that dress and they won't last long anyway."

"That's what you think," I mumbled.

Chloe had spent her time staring out the window. "Look, you'd be proud of me, I found a skateboard."

I looked out and saw what she was talking about, a long line of stars with two placed beneath them where the wheels would be.

"You'll be an astronomer yet," I said.

She turned to me, looked me over. "You look great. And it's not really fair, I had to pop out two kids to get half your curves."

I laughed because to me, she looked great in her slim, petite frame.

"Let's go."

I watched as she pressed the wall to open the door, then we turned right to walk down a long, beige corridor.

"We're in the living quarters. You can tell by the brown and orange colors on the walls. That set of colors is for civilian areas." She slid her hand along the stripe in the center of the metal wall as she went. "Engineering's blue, medical areas are green, communications are white, command is black and battle stations are red."

No way I was going to remember all of that. "What do you do with the I.C., exactly?" I had an idea, but she said Ronan worked with her, and I was not above prying for more information to help me understand my mates.

We turned another corner and I peeked over my shoulder, seeing where we'd come from in the hopes of remembering my way back. Everything looked the same.

"I can't really talk about it, sorry. If the commander gives me clearance, I'll spill. Until then, I can't say a word. War stuff."

"Okay. And Ronan?"

Her look was sympathetic but she didn't give me any answers. "I probably already told you too much."

Damn. Fine. I'd try a different track. "So, you were a bride. I assume you were matched, too? Warden Egara?"

She nodded and stopped in front of what I thought was an elevator. Others passed us and Chloe nodded to them. Some looked like Kaed and Ronan, all toffee colored and huge. None of the males were less than six feet tall. Some I recognized as Atlans, big, but not beastly. At least not at the moment.

Clearly, they grew guys bigger in space.

"Yes, to Seth Mills—he's human, by the way—and Dorian

Kanaker. He's Prillon and the reason for this gold collar. I've been here a few years. Have two little rugrats, Dara is two and a half. She's human. And her little brother just started walking. Christopher. He's Dorian's, and already an overly protective brother even though he can barely walk straight."

Her face lit up when she mentioned them. I felt a pang of envy.

"How do your mates do, with that?"

"What?"

"With knowing they aren't the father of one of your children."

Chloe scoffed at me as if I'd insulted her. "Try telling Dorian that Dara isn't his daughter, and you'll find out for yourself." She softened her scolding with a grin. "But I wouldn't recommend it."

The doors opened and it was an elevator—as suspected. We stepped on and took us up. Somewhere.

"Can I ask you something?" Chloe asked.

I glanced down at her, nodded. "Sure."

"You don't have to answer, but I'm curious. You're not wearing your collar. Did you take it off? I want to warn you, Karter and Ronan are total cavemen, so they might be upset with you for taking it off. Prillon warriors tend to be a bit overbearing and possessive. In fact, I'm surprised they didn't already sense that you're not wearing it."

I took a deep breath, let it out. "They didn't give me one."

Her mouth fell open and her eyes were wide. "What?"

The elevator door opened and when two huge blue guys in black uniforms just like Karter wore tried to step forward, Chloe held up her hand and stopped them in their tracks. "Take the next one."

"What kind of alien was that?" I'd read every brochure in the processing center and not read one word about blue aliens that were seven feet tall.

The door slid shut and she turned to face me. "Xerima. Their planet is considered primitive, like Earth. But they're very aggressive and hard to control. Good for fighting the Hive, bad for being holed up in a battleship. Those two are here as test cases."

"Test cases? What does that mean?"

"They're new. If they work out, Fleet Command will allow more of them to serve. If not, they go home and go back to—whatever it is they do there. But don't change the subject."

Okay then…

"What do you mean they didn't give you a collar? That's what Prillon mates do. They give a collar to their female so no one will try to make a move on their mate, and so you're all… connected."

I shrugged when she gaped. I had no explanation or theory, none that I wanted to speak out loud.

"How do they know what you want in bed?"

Good god, did this woman have *no* boundaries? "Kaed says it's not safe for him to have a mate. That he works too much and it's too dangerous for us to be connected like that."

"He's giving you up?" Her voice went up in stunned surprise.

I shrugged. "I don't know. Do Prillons have one-night stands?"

"One night—" She blinked at me. "You think they fucked you and forgot about you? No way."

Her hand swiped through the air and she completely missed my wince at her words… *fucked you and forgot about you.* Yes. That seemed pretty standard from where I was sitting. First on Earth, now here.

When the elevator door opened again, she sighed, tugged my arm and pulled me off, letting people in green uniforms on. The walls here were the same green, and if I remembered what Chloe said, we were in the medical area. "No, Erica. No way. I've known Karter for years. There is no way he'd pull something that stupid."

"I don't know what is going on with him, but still... I came all this way for a mate. Two, it seems, and now Kaed won't give me his collar. Even Ronan is mad at him."

"I don't get it." She sounded stunned. "Did they even... I mean, did you guys... you know? I assumed, earlier. I mean, you were naked. So I just assumed."

"Yes," I replied, leaning down so those walking by didn't hear. "*That* was crazy. But it wasn't what I wanted, either. It wasn't like what I saw when Warden Egara tested me. I was hoping for too much, I guess. There's a difference between a dream and real life."

"God, I loved that testing chair. I hear you." We shared a glance of feminine understanding before she looked away, steering me around a very large Atlan warrior who seemed in a big hurry to get somewhere.

She pursed her lips together, studied me. "Let's finish our tour." She looked around. "God, where the hell are we?"

Going back to the wall, she called the elevator, slapping her hand on it as if she were mad.

"We'll go on the tour. I'll drop you off in the mess hall so you can eat, then I'm going to have a little chat with your mate."

I didn't argue. Didn't want to. If she could talk some sense into the stubborn Commander Makaed Karter, I was *not* going to be the one to stop her.

CHAPTER 10

Ronan, Battleship Karter, Command Deck, Karter's Office

Frustration bubbled inside me like magma boiling in my gut. The probe was worthless. Fucking worthless. Commander Varsten. His battleship. His warriors.

Gone.

For fucking nothing.

For one moment I understood why Kaed refused to give Erica a collar. This rage burning inside me should never touch something so beautiful as our mate. With Kaed's emotional turmoil added to mine? She'd melt into a puddle on the floor and beg us to let her go.

Neither of us would be able to do that. Not after last night, her soft curves in my hands, her wet heat wrapped around my cock as her pussy milked me of my seed. She could, at this very moment, be carrying a child. Our child. Being locked to our minds would be a special kind of torture. I understood that now.

"There has so be something in that data. Look again." I.C.

Commander Chloe Phan's narrowed eyes and cold voice spoke volumes. She felt it, too. Helpless.

We'd had the probe for several hours, checked every piece of data, and it gave us nothing. We all knew Sector 437—and Battlegroup Karter—had to be next. *We* would be next.

The data tech who'd programmed the encryption codes into the probe prior to launch shook her head. She was one of Varsten's best, and even she looked helpless and defeated. "I'm sorry. Everything on the probe was functioning at optimal levels. Whatever new tech the Hive are using to hide from us is working."

"We're screwed." Chloe crossed her arms, her foot tapping a constant, steady beat on the hard floor. "We need to start evacuating non-essential personnel. While we don't have definitive data, we need to be smart. I need to report this to Core Command."

The probe tech looked at Commander Karter for permission to leave. At his nod, she left the room, Bard and a handful of others following. They all had their orders. There was no way in hell we were going to do exactly what the Varsten had done—get everyone we could off this ship and try to lure the Hive close enough to figure out what they were hitting us with.

Dangerous game. One I'd played before. "All due respect, Commander, but trying to bait a trap didn't work for Varsten. You know that."

Kaed looked at me, nodded. "I know. Which is why I've already spoken to Prime Nial. He's re-routing three battlegroups to this location. We can't retreat; we have to hold this sector. But with the additional ships and warriors, we'll be able to block grid this sector and search every single inch of it. When we're done, we'll go back to Varsten's sector and start over. We aren't going to sit here and wait for them to hit us."

"How long before the additional ships arrive?" I asked.

"Two days. Based on the timeline of the previous Hive attacks, we should have time to find them before they can hit the Karter."

"Jesus, I hope you're right." Chloe sighed, her arms crossed. It was the best we could do and we all knew it. With heavily populated planets so close to our sector, we could not abandon this area of space. Retreat was not an option.

"I'm sending out scout ships as we speak, everything we've got. And we need to use all non-combat vessels for civilian evacuations. We need to get our people clear of the battle zone *and* empty our landing bays to make room for additional fighter pilots and their ships." Kaed was staring at schematics and data streaming across his desk, his voice matter-of-fact, but I knew him well enough to know he was relieved reinforcements were on the way.

Gods knew I was. All I could think about was Erica. Where was she? Was she safe? Hungry? Happy? Aroused? Did she miss me?

If she were wearing my collar, I'd know how she was feeling no matter where she was on this ship. I wanted that connection. Needed it. Now that I'd been in her arms, touched her warmth, I felt cold without her. Empty.

And mere seconds ago I'd been thinking about how the chaos of my mind would be torture for her.

Having a mate was making me lose my fucking mind.

"And your mate?" Chloe asked, as if she'd been reading my thoughts.

Commander Karter used his command voice, and it was neither friendly nor interested in arguments. "She needs to be escorted to a shuttle at once, for immediate evacuation. I won't have her in danger."

"You going to talk to her first?" Chloe challenged him anyway. By the gods, these Earth females truly were fearless.

"No need. She will understand."

"Fuck, that's harsh." Chloe's boot picked up the pace, tapping faster and faster as her lips thinned in disapproval. "You're making a huge mistake, Commander."

I glanced from Kaed to Commander Chloe Phan. So much power in such a small body. She was human, like my mate. Like Prime Nial's mate, Jessica. Lady Jessica Deston, mate of Nial and Ander, was also from Earth. And she wore the Prime's collar. She was well known throughout the entire Coalition Fleet for being calm and calculating under pressure. Most Prillon warriors who met her, adored her. And she had the undying loyalty of every single warrior banished to the Colony. She'd fought and won the right for them to have mates of their own.

Surely Prime Nial's mental agony could rival mine or Kaed's?

If so, it would seem females from Earth were stronger than they looked. Surely this would be true for Erica as well.

But I would not argue with Kaed in front of this female, Chloe Phan of Earth. She was not mine. She was not family. "I'll report to Core Command," I offered.

Chloe looked up at me, an assessing gaze I'd not seen from her before. "Fine. But before the shit hits the fan out here, and one of you gets yourself killed, you two better set things right with your mate."

That got Kaed's attention. And mine.

"Our mate is well and has been properly cared for, I assure you," Kaed said. I held my tongue, waiting for the explosion I knew was coming. Commander Chloe Phan did not drop that kind of warning without something of substance behind her words.

"I believe she would disagree."

Boom.

"What?" The commander was in full form now, leaning

forward, his status as a caring and honorable Prillon warrior being challenged by the petite human female. Me? I was not surprised. I had not challenged Kaed's decision to spare Erica the mental anguish of wearing our collars, but I also knew our mate well enough already to know she would not be satisfied with such an arrangement.

"She's right, Commander Karter." We shouldn't have touched her last night. Fuck, that would have been almost impossible, but we could have done it. Instead of fucking her to exhaustion, we should have let her go, given her to another who would not hesitate to bond himself and his second to her in a full claiming. I couldn't believe the words flew from my mouth, but they were true. I deliberately called him by his command name, and not his nickname. That name was for family. Something neither of us had any business wanting.

Kaed held up his large hand, blocking my face from his view as he stared at Chloe. "Explain. Now."

"She wants your collar, Commander. She was tested at the Interstellar Brides Processing center, just like every other bride gifted to Prillon warriors. She already knows what it's going to feel like to have a collar around her neck when you claim her, how all of your emotions and needs and lust will bleed together into one glorious, overwhelming explosion of pleasure." As Chloe spoke, her eyes practically rolled into her head as memories of being claimed by her two warriors must have filled her mind. "She won't accept less. And if you can't give her everything, you should give her to someone who can, before she loves you any more than she already does."

"She loves me?"

Chloe opened her eyes, the softness and desire I had witnessed there fading so quickly I questioned whether or not I had actually seen them.

"She loves you both, idiots. Earth women don't go carnal

GRACE GOODWIN

and submissive unless they want you, and *trust you.* Being naked, taking you inside our bodies, it's an act of trust. Commitment. She said she could already be pregnant. She's all in, giving you everything, and you're not living up to your end of the bargain. You are *not* giving her what was promised."

Karter stepped back as if in shock. "I was tested years ago. I was new to my command. I had no idea what kind of life I would have as commander of this ship."

"Day late and a dollar short."

I frowned. "What does that mean?"

She sighed and looked at me as Karter lowered his hand. "It means, it's too late. From the testing, she knows what it feels like to have a collar around her neck and be claimed by two males who are delirious with desire and love and need. She's *felt it before.*" Chloe walked toward the door, and I didn't have the heart to stop her. I'd heard enough, my heart aching as if she'd stabbed me with a rounded blade from the dining room.

But she wasn't done with us. Not yet.

She spun about to face us. "She's felt it all, just *not* with the two of you." The door slid open and there stood our dissatisfied mate, Bard at her side, serving as escort. She looked beautiful in a brown Prillon gown. Curved. Soft. Perfect. She smiled in greeting, but the light didn't reach her eyes, and I knew Chloe had spoken the truth. Erica was not happy, even with all the pleasure we'd given her. She would not choose to stay with us if we didn't surrender everything.

I broke, my insides cracking and withering to dust at the idea of losing her.

She could have me. All of me. Heart. Mind. Soul. I'd lay my sins at her feet and beg her to heal me with her soft touch and wet heat. She was light to my darkness. I didn't want to exist without her, not now that I'd tasted her, known bliss, the slide of her hot pussy over my cock, her scent, the sounds of her pleasure, the way she'd clung to me in sleep. *Mine.*

That fast, I knew I would do anything to make her happy. She belonged to me. And if she wanted to feel my desire, feel the need burning through my veins like lightning, I would not deny her. I would resign from the Fleet if I had to, take her home to Prillon Prime and spend my days chasing children and my nights making her scream with pleasure. I'd served my time. I'd fought and bled and suffered for years... for her.

Fuck. I couldn't lose her.

If Karter didn't want to give her everything, I'd name a second and keep her for myself.

ommander Karter

've been mad before. Frustrated. Angry. I'd learned to control it all the way back in the Coalition Academy. No commander could lead if every one of his—or her—emotions were known. Who wanted to obey the commands of a leader who was out of control?

But the Hive had nothing on Erica Roberts from Earth. She riled something hidden within, as if the matching protocol had found some kind of button inside me and it had been pushed. Now. Years after my testing. By a female I'd known less than a day.

By my *mate.*

The door to my office slid silently open and Erica entered, accompanied by Bard. I was thankful she was with my second-in-command, content that she was well-protected. She did not wear my collar, and I would not have any horny warrior panting after what was mine. While everyone on the ship—perhaps the entire battlegroup—knew of my mating, I would kill any who dared look upon her with lust. I stood, taking every inch of her in. Of course my cock went hard at the sight of her in a traditional Prillon dress in a dark, rich brown.

The Karter family color, the color my collar would turn if Ronan and I claimed her in the traditional way, the way she wanted us to.

Her golden brown hair hung past her shoulders, her blue eyes fastened on me, assessing, not placid nor appeased by my presence, as I wished her to be.

The long, flowing material of the gown, while not overly revealing or sexual, revealed every one of her lush curves. She looked refreshed, her eyes bright, the exhaustion I'd seen on her face as she slept, gone as well.

I'd waited for Ronan to sleep, then turned, watching her face at rest for long hours, wondering at this completely unexpected turn my life had taken. I was not young. I was older than most of the warriors still fighting. I'd seen more than twenty years of battle, more than forty years of life. Everyone I'd known or loved, dead or long gone. Even Ronan, or so I'd believed, until yesterday.

A mate. Gods help me. What the fuck was I supposed to do now?

She eyed me, then Ronan, who had also stood.

I knew how those eyes became hooded when she came, how they lost their focus as she found her pleasure on my cock. I knew the hot, tight feel of her pussy as it milked the cum from my balls and she cried out, losing control.

"Mate," I growled. She licked her lips at my tone. I saw her shiver and knew it wasn't from being cold. It hadn't been long since we'd first fucked her, and I could imagine our combined seed sliding down her thighs. I wanted her to feel our possession of her even now, even when we weren't touching her. Despite the fact that her neck was bare, her body responded to me, and we were fully clothed.

And yet Chloe claimed my mate hadn't been satisfied? Two Prillon warriors had left her disappointed, even after what we'd done with her? And worse, she'd spoken of her dissatisfaction with Chloe?

Not only did it stir up every one of my leadership instincts to fix the problem—it was in my nature to ensure my people were satisfied—but it also pushed my mating instincts to full strength. I needed to ensure her happiness, both in bed and out.

"Commander Karter." She nodded in my direction, *nodded.*

"Commander Wothar."

I settled when Ronan received the same treatment from our female. No wonder Atlans turned beast. I felt as if I was coming out of my skin, as if I wanted to grab her, kiss her, get in her, fuck her, claim her with an intensity that was terrifying in its mindless demand.

I'd given in to her request and broken the custom of only the primary mate fucking her pussy and planting his seed until pregnancy was assured. She'd wanted both of us to fuck her, to fill her with a child. Ronan had combined his seed with mine deep inside her. A baby would be *ours.* I'd even given in to her request and kept her on the Karter with me as we awaited data from the probe, even with the possibility of danger. Not just danger, being blown from space by some long-range Hive weapon. But now?

Now we suspected the Hive would move to Sector 437 next. Battlegroup Karter *would* be next.

As I stared at my mate, non-essential personnel were already being transported off the forward ships, others in the battlegroup moved to safety, just as Varsten had ordered.

And once I proved to Erica that her mates could well and truly satisfy her every need, she would be transported to safety. To Prime Nial himself. His mate, Jessica, was also a female from Earth and would ease Erica's transition to Prillon Prime. Erica would be wined and dined and sleep in silken sheets while I battled the Hive. While Ronan went off and did fuck-all with the I.C.

She would know the satisfaction only her mates could give her, and then we would see her transported safely to the home planet. We would master her body and ensure her safety as any good mates would.

Starting right now.

I strode toward her and she took a step back, eyes widening. Then again until she was pressed up against the wall. I crowded against her, my hard cock pressing into the softness of her belly. Reaching up, I tangled my fingers in her long hair, tugged gently so she had no choice but to meet my gaze. She was pinned in place.

"Chloe, out," I snapped. "Take Bard with you."

"Okay then," Chloe said behind me.

I hadn't shifted my gaze off of Erica from the second she walked in. The air in the room crackled like the air on Prillon Prime before a lightning strike.

Out of the corner of my eye, I saw Chloe walk over to Bard, grab his arm and tug him toward the door. "Have fun!" she called as the door closed behind them.

"I like seeing you in traditional Prillon dress," I said. Even more, I loved seeing her in my family color. Brown. Rich. Soft. Full of life.

Like her.

She licked her lips, whispered, "Thank you."

"It is a shame I will rip it to shreds, but the S-Gen machine can make you another."

"What?" she asked. "Why? I like this dress."

I gave her hair a little tug. Nothing painful, but it was time to assert my dominance. I was her primary male and she would know that. "Because we have learned from Commander Phan that you have not been properly satisfied."

She did not deny it, and my cock pulsed with pain.

"Kaed, I just—"

"It is our fault," Ronan said from behind me. He moved to stand beside us as he traced the line of her neck with a finger. He touched her, but his eyes were on me, the question—no, demand—clear. He wanted to collar her. Here. Now.

She shivered again, and I knew she would let us take her with or without the collar. "We are going to make sure you know who your mates are, female." My hand roamed the softness of her hip and outer thigh, moved up to cup her large breast. I wanted to rip the dress to shreds to reach her bare skin.

"We didn't realize how needy your pussy was," Ronan added, correctly interpreting my lack of an answer *as* my answer. We'd fuck her now, get her to safety, and figure out the rest later. My feelings on burdening Erica with my emotions had not changed. I carried darkness and death. I did not wish that for her.

"My—what? No, that's not what I meant."

"Perhaps you were matched to us because you needed not one mate, but two. We can satisfy your insatiable need," I vowed.

"Here?" she squeaked. "Anyone could walk in."

She wasn't denying her need, or protesting the fact that we would fuck her... dominate her, here and now. But she didn't want us to be discovered. For now. I had no doubt she would not mind being witnessed, for the testing would not have matched us had she felt otherwise.

Ronan reached out, slapped the wall beside the door and engaged the lock. This would be the only concession we made.

"She will need her dress. After," Ronan reminded me, not stating that she would transport immediately after, and neither of us wanted her to be naked. Even being sent to the ruler of all of Prillon Prime, I would not send her vulnerable and bare. Showing her off while fucking, letting others see the beautiful female that was ours and ours alone, was one thing.

It was tradition for an Interstellar Bride to arrive to her Prillon warriors naked and unashamed. But now that she was mine, I found myself increasingly unwilling to share her beauty with the rest of the galaxy.

Ronan was right. I would not tear her dress, for I had no S-Gen machine in my office to prepare her a replacement. Grabbing the long hem, I raised the dress, higher and higher still until it bunched in the front at her waist. With the hand I removed from her hair, I cupped her pussy, found it bare. Wet. Despite what I'd thought, the thick smears of seed that had coated her last night were gone, even along her inner thighs.

I growled and her eyes, which had fallen closed, flared wide at the sound.

"Your pussy is empty, mate," I said. "Where is our seed?"

"I... I took a shower." She gasped and rolled her hips as I slipped one finger inside her, reveled in how she responded.

"Really?" I asked, slipping my hand from between her legs. "To erase our touch from your body? To forget whose bed you slept in last night?"

"No." Her mouth fell open, then her eyes changed. The

haze of lust lifted as they narrowed and went cold. "What is your problem, Kaed?"

"You speak of being unhappy, mate. But not with us, your mates. With Chloe Phan, an outsider. She is not a member of this family. She is not ours."

Erica shoved at my chest, but I did not move. Not one inch.

"You sent her to me. A friend from Earth. You expect me not to speak of being here? It's not like I told her how big your cocks are. I do have some discretion."

"Tell us what you need," Ronan said. "We will fix it."

"How? You think a good, hard fuck will solve all my problems?" Erica's fury spiked, as did her heart rate, the scent of her arousal filling my office to the point that even Ronan growled.

I grabbed her hand, pulled her over to my desk. With an aggressive swipe, I cleared the surface, picked her up and sat her upon it.

"We will not leave here until this is resolved," I said.

"You have all the answers. Know everything. Why should you consult me? I'm just your perfect match, your bride, the woman good enough to fuck but not good enough to marry."

"Mate," I growled, pushed to my limit. I would never harm a female, never harm my mate, but she was pushing me. "I do not know what marry means, but you are my *mate.*"

"Are you sure about that?"

"Our seed in your womb makes us sure," Ronan added.

Her cheeks flushed a bright pink.

"Explain your concerns, mate," I repeated, trying to slow this down, get myself under control.

She crossed her arms over her chest in a stubborn gesture I'd seen Chloe do. I had to wonder if her mates felt as I did now.

"You might both be commanders, but you can't boss *me* around."

I looked to Ronan, who nodded.

"Perhaps a good spanking will get you to answer us," I replied.

I lifted her with ease and flipped her over so she was bent over my desk.

With Ronan's hand on her upper back, he held her down when she tried to push up.

"Hey!" she shouted.

The bottom of her dress was tossed up and bunched at her lower back, exposing her bare, glorious ass. I spanked her once. Not hard, but enough so she knew I would follow through.

Her hips wiggled as my handprint bloomed bright pink on her pale skin. As she thrashed her legs about, her pussy became visible. I had to adjust my cock in my pants.

"You are satisfied with our cocks. I can see your pussy is swollen and dripping with heat. Do you see how hard her clit is, Ronan? Is that it, mate? You need to come again?"

"Do you need Kaed's big cock, Erica?" Ronan asked, stroking her hair back from her face.

"Men! You think everything can be solved by sex. This is not about your dicks."

I slid two fingers deep into her pussy and she moaned, pushing back against me, trying to force my touch deeper. I complied, eager to see if she was truly disinterested. I knew her wetness could be attributed to our earlier play and not her current arousal. I doubted that, but I would make sure. I would not fuck her if she were not willing.

To my surprise, and perhaps hers as well, she came, her inner walls clenching rhythmically around my fingers. She cried out my name as her hands slapped the desk.

"By the gods, Kaed," Ronan whispered, watching. "She is magnificent."

"Let me up," she gasped.

Stunned by her powerful response, we let her up, but she surprised us once more by spinning about, dropping to her knees before me and tugging open my uniform pants. With eager hands, she pulled my cock out and pumped it once, twice, causing me to stumble back. She followed until I ran into the wall. This time, I was the one trapped. She had my cock in her small hands; I wasn't going anywhere.

I shouted her name when she leaned forward and put the wide crown into her mouth. "This," she said, after a swirl of her tongue. "Do you feel this with others?"

I barely had brain function as she continued to pump and lick. Just seeing her on her knees, my cock in her hold... fuck. "What?"

"Do other females make pre-cum slide from you?" she flicked her tongue over a pearly drop.

"Mate, you doubt our honor?" Ronan asked.

She offered him a glance. "Do you doubt mine?"

She took me deep, although there was no way she would ever be able to take all of me. Her fist around the base kept me from going too deep, but gods, the hot, wet suction was making me lose my mind. I couldn't think, couldn't speak, couldn't function with her mouth on me. The Hive could break through the locked door and I wouldn't be able to respond.

And so, with a willpower stronger than I'd ever used before, I gripped her under the arms and lifted her up, sat her on the desk once again.

The air was cool on my wet dick and my balls ached for release.

"You think we doubt your honor?" I asked.

Her chin tipped up. "Well, something is obviously wrong with me."

"You are perfect, female." I meant it. Perfect.

"I don't wear your collar."

Ah, that was it. She must have seen a Prillon claiming in her testing dream, knew of the collar's importance.

"You arrived from Earth in the midst of death and destruction."

"I'm not afraid of death," she replied. "I came out here for a reason, Kaed."

I felt... proud of her in that moment, realized she hadn't been the least bit panicked at her odd arrival. She'd jumped right in, offering help to the wounded, even if it were just holding a hand, giving a smile and words of encouragement to our injured warriors. She hadn't feared the danger. But I had, for her.

"No, you were not." I tipped my head toward Ronan. "Neither is your second. But with your lack of fear comes my responsibility. I am the leader of this battlegroup, Erica. My life is wracked with guilt, grief, anger. Hatred. So many negative feelings would come through the collar, just from me alone, that I am not sure you would survive a connection to both of us with your mind intact."

She frowned. "I could die? Are you telling me that if you two put your collar around my neck, it might kill me? Because I'm calling bullshit on that one."

"No, but sometimes, perhaps you will wish you had. The collars connect us, Erica. Not just sexual pleasure, but all emotion. The good *and* the bad. I will not burden you with a connection to me. To what I must endure in my role as a fleet commander. As for Ronan... I can only imagine the pain and depth of feeling he's had from being in the I.C."

"You don't know either, you can only imagine," she countered. "With the collars, you'd know."

"I can handle his energy, for it is a twin to mine, no doubt. But you won't be able to handle that kind of burden from both of us. I won't allow you to endure it."

She hopped down, went around the desk and paced. "You won't *allow it?* Who made you the decision maker? We've been matched. We've been mated. The testing would have given you a mate who can handle whatever you have to offer."

Ah, her words rang true. My mate was not weak, but strong. Perhaps too strong. "I will not allow you to *handle* the burdens of my command."

"We are at a stalemate then," she replied. Ah, was she fierce. There wasn't a meek bone in her body. "Perhaps I will have to change your mind."

Her gaze dropped to my cock, which was still hard. It wouldn't go down until I came deep inside her. And then, I wondered if even that would tame my need.

"You think to fuck me into compliance?" I asked.

"That's what you tried to do to me." Her arms crossed over her chest again.

The corner of Ronan's mouth tipped up, and I didn't need to read his mind. She was right. We had.

"And you wished to suck my cock for mine," I asked.

She arched a brow, not denying it.

"So we drown in sex until one of us compromises," she offered.

I looked to Ronan who only arched a blond brow. She was being transported to Prillon Prime and Prime Nial the moment we took her to the transport room. The coordinates had been set.

She understood now why I refused to collar her. That seemed to be enough to appease her, at least for the moment. A détente in this one topic. If she was this angry about the collar, shipping her off to safety would not be met with happiness. She would fight me on that decision as well. I could easily overpower her, force her to leave, which might become necessary. Her safety was not up for any kind of compromise or negotiation.

And so I would take this time before she hated me to have her again. To sink into the feelings of being with Erica, *in* Erica, the pleasure I felt even without a collar. For when I set her on the transport and gave the order to the tech, she would hate me. Perhaps even choose another mate before her return from our homeworld.

But she would be safe and that was all that mattered.

I curled my finger, beckoning her over. With my other hand, I gripped my cock and stroked it. She came toward me slowly, her gaze on my moving hand.

"You have two mates. Two cocks to satisfy."

She looked to Ronan, who'd remained quiet and watchful through our argument.

I grabbed my desk chair, which had been knocked out of the way, dropped into it, continuing to stroke my hard length. "Lift up that dress and climb on."

Her eyes widened and I watched as she transformed from disgruntled and aggravated mate back to aroused and eager. Her temper flared as hot as her pussy.

We watched as she slowly lifted the dress. Ronan opened his pants, pulled out his cock. She moved close, ready to climb into my lap.

I shook my head. "Turn around."

A little frown formed, but she complied. I grabbed her hips, saw my handprint still on her ass. "This way."

She caught on quickly, backing up and sitting on my lap, getting her legs positioned over mine, facing away from me. Her feet didn't touch the ground so I gripped her hips, lifted her up so I could align my cock at her entrance, then lowered her down. She surrounded me, one hot, tight inch at a time.

Ronan moved to lean his hips against my desk.

Only when I was fully seated did I use my feet to wheel my chair closer to Ronan. He spread his legs wide so I could move close, so close that Erica was aligned perfectly to tip her head down and suck Ronan off.

She did. She sucked. I fucked. Ronan tugged at her hair.

We didn't last. None of us could hold back our orgasms. We'd been primed, eager. I'd heard of make-up sex from Chloe, but had never experienced it before. The intensity of it. The shared need. But it was even more powerful now, for Ronan and I both knew we would be sending her away. This would be the last time we were together like this for a while. Perhaps she sensed our tinge of desperation, for she came with a moan, nothing more, for she was swallowing as much of Ronan's cock as she could.

Her inner walls milked and clenched, dripped her arousal all over me.

And that had me coming, filling her, my cum seemingly never ending.

Ronan growled, bucked his hips up and I watched her throat work to take it all.

She lifted her head, licked him clean as I raised her up and pulled out, held her close as Ronan righted his pants. I handed her off when he was done and did the same. She was quiet and compliant. Thank the gods. And I loved seeing her like this. Content. Sated.

Coated in my seed.

We stood, went out of my office and down the corridor. She didn't question where we were headed, probably because she thought we were returning to our quarters for more.

But we weren't. She only stirred when we were almost to the transport room.

"This isn't the family area. The wall isn't brown."

We didn't say anything, just went into the transport room

and right up onto the pad. "Lock in coordinates to Prillon Prime as previously directed," I ordered.

Ronan kissed the top of her head. "Ronan!" she said, quickly understanding.

I went up to her, kissed her. "Your safety is crucial. We can't do our jobs if we worry about you, about a possible child."

"Wait a minute, you can't send me back to Earth!"

"You are going to Prillon Prime where you will be safe until this battle is over."

"I should be with you," she countered.

Ronan stepped off the pad. I took one step back and she followed. Holding out my hand, I stopped her, kept her on the pad.

"Engage transport lock," I said, yanking my hand back. I knew she'd resist and had prepared for this, warned the tech to be ready to use the transport lock which kept whomever was transporting from leaving the pad. It was used for criminals, or those we needed to ensure wouldn't refuse transport, or to ensure they went from one pad to the next without incident.

I had to wonder if it had been used on a mate before, but I would see her safe. She would be with Prime Nial in seconds.

Ronan stood at my side as she called our names. I ached to grab her, pull her into my arms again, but it was not to be. I was responsible for her safety and that came over my need for her. We'd only had her a day and now we would be separated.

"We will come for you as soon as it is safe."

"Kaed!" she cried. "Damn it, no!"

"Transport," I growled, and watched her disappear before my eyes.

CHAPTER 11

Erica, Prillon Prime, Transport Room #27

At least when I transported this time, I came through in my dress. I might be an astronomer, but I wasn't up on transporting. Molecules bending. Wormholes or something. Why Earth clothing—even the ugly IBP gown— hadn't materialized when I'd come from the testing center, I had no idea.

Now was not the time to wonder more. Like *Harry Potter* and the flue powder, I was almost immediately somewhere new. The room looked identical, but Kaed and Ronan weren't here. The transport tech was someone else and a pretty woman —a human woman—was standing at the bottom of the steps.

"You're here! Yay!" She clapped her hands together in her excitement.

When I made my way off the pad, she pulled me into her arms. For once, there was a woman taller than me. If I had to guess, I'd say she was about six feet tall. She appeared younger, more slender and had gorgeous blonde hair. She looked like she could be either a runway model or a beach volleyball player. She wore a similar dress to mine, but hers was in a dark red that matched the collar around her neck. It seemed women who were matched from Earth were huggers.

"I'm Jessica."

The tech bowed to her as we walked by and she leaned in close. "I'm also Lady Deston. Prime Nial is one of my mates and he's the ruler of the planet and the entire Coalition Fleet. Fancy, right? But I'm from the states, served in the military and I eat with a fork and knife like everyone else. I don't feel all that fancy."

She took a deep breath and laughed. "Sorry, you'd think I haven't talked in a while. It's just that you're from Earth and we're rare up here. I'm excited for some girl time."

"Thanks," I replied, although I didn't feel much like girl time. I felt like kicking ass and taking names. I thought back to Chloe's choice of clothing from earlier. Maybe I should have selected the fighter uniform after all. I wanted the thigh holster and space weapon now so I could hold the transport tech up and force him to send me back. Then shoot my mates for being idiots.

"Where exactly am I?" I asked.

Her mouth opened, then closed. "You don't know?"

I laughed. "I was on the transport pad, coordinates locked in before I knew what was happening."

She frowned after hearing my answer. "Well, you're on Prillon Prime. Karter contacted Nial and requested you stay here while they deal with the Hive weapon. I thought you would know, be... prepared or something. It's not like you need a suitcase up here with S-Gen machines, but still." She paused, studied me. "You're safe, at least. You don't look scared of the battleship being blown out of the sky. In fact, you look... angry. You're mad because Karter and your second want you safe?"

I glanced over my shoulder at the tech, and Jessica took my arm and led me out into the hallway. Just as unexciting as on the battleship.

"Spill, girlfriend."

I glanced at her collar, the dark red completely different than Chloe's gold. I put my hand to my bare neck and Jessica's gaze followed the gesture. Her eyes widened.

"You're not collared." She put her hand on my arm. "Holy shit, did you refuse Karter's claim? Are you going to ask for a different mate?"

I shook my head. "No, I want Kaed and Ronan."

She frowned. "Okaaaay. Then why—"

"He won't give it to me."

"What, the collar?" Her mouth fell open. "Are you serious? I mean, Prillon males are ridiculously possessive. I'm surprised he let you out of his sight, let alone transport off his ship without being claimed. Nial would have been here with me now to meet you, but he's working with Karter and the other commanders on the plan to get more ships out there and find the new Hive weapon. And Ander, my second, is with them."

"Yeah, but you've got the collar," I pointed out. "No one is going to jump you."

I didn't think anyone was going to jump me either. If Karter wasn't keen on keeping me, what Prillon would be?

"*Did* Karter jump you? I mean, it's just the collar he refused, not you, right?"

I couldn't help but blush because it felt like fifteen minutes ago I was being well-fucked by him and Ronan. Together. Not felt, it *had* been only fifteen minutes ago. They'd given me an amazing orgasm and used that to their advantage, getting me onto the transport pad before I'd fully recovered.

"Don't worry, he's not *that* disinterested." I felt his seed sliding down my thighs as I replied. "Seems no man—regardless of what planet they're from—can say no to a woman who wants him naked."

"And you want them? You want to keep them?"

"Yes. I do. Stubborn jerks."

She stomped her foot. "Still, this isn't right. You're here and he's there and you have no collar. No one knows you belong to him on Prillon Prime. I'm sure up on the Karter, it's well-known." Crossing her arms over her chest, she added, "I don't think we should let him get away with this, do you?"

"No," I grumbled. "I want to go back to the Karter and give him a piece of my mind."

"Damn it. This is hard." She reached out her hand and took mine with a gentle squeeze. "I don't blame you for being angry, but your ship might be attacked at any time. I know he sent you here without asking, but he is thinking of your safety."

"From what I've been told, a battleship can *always* be attacked. Karter and Ronan are *always* going to be working, fighting the Hive." Even though we were just outside the transport room in a hallway, I began to pace. "I was matched to him. The testing had to know a Prillon warrior's job would always be to fight, to face possible death. It's no different from being married to a soldier or a police officer back home. There are no guarantees in life, Jessica. The matching protocol had to know I could handle it, even if Karter doesn't want me to. Ronan, too."

She studied me, cocked her head. "I never thought of it that way, but you're right. It's the entire philosophy behind their tradition of choosing a second."

"Exactly."

"Why would the testing match you to a mate or a situation you could not handle? You belong with them."

I sighed, then smiled. "I'm so glad you think so. I thought I was the only one. Chloe's with the I.C. and she's still up there. She fights for Pete's sake. Goes out into battle. I mean, look at me, it's not like I'm going to tip over in the wind. I'm sturdy. Strong. I can handle this. I *need* to. Commander Phan said I was Lady Karter and in charge of all non-military stuff on the ship."

"That is true. As the Commander's mate, you would be elevated to a place of honor and responsibility within his battlegroup."

"I can't do anything helpful from here."

"No, you can't." She grabbed my arm again, tugged me back into the transport room. The tech bowed to her again. "Set the transporter to return coordinates on Battleship Karter. Lady Karter is going home."

The tech raised a dark brow but remained quiet. Jessica copied the motion and didn't say a word. I watched both of them, clearly a silent battle happening in front of me. Jessica was Lady Deston, mated to the leader of Prillon Prime and the entire Interplanetary Coalition. Her mates, Nial and Ander, were in charge of the entire Coalition Fleet. She could probably order Kaed and Ronan both to do whatever she wanted.

The transport tech didn't stand a chance. Yet he was military, so did that mean he was to report up to Prime Nial, her mate?

"Now," she added, which got the desired effect.

"Yes, Lady Deston." He nodded to me to proceed onto the platform.

Guess that answered that.

I felt the now-familiar vibrations beneath my feet, felt the hairs on my arms rise.

She grabbed me in a fierce hug. "Go. Be with your mates. We'll see each other again soon."

I'd been here five minutes and I knew I had an ally—and a friend—in Jessica. "Thank you."

"Transport ready, Lady Deston," the tech said.

I went up onto the pad, looked to Jessica. She curled her fingers in a little wave, but she was gone before I could wave back.

Commander Karter

"**S**tatus update," I said, hands on hips.

The flight bay had three levels of decks, cargo and evac ships readying on each of them. From our location on the docking control station, we could monitor each deck, see the ships as they were being maintained and processed for use. Beyond was the invisible environmental shield, the powerful barrier that maintained our air and oxygen levels and other essentials for life to function. With no exterior wall, it was as if someone could walk across the deck and jump into space. Nothing but blackness and stars were beyond.

The bay's activity was higher than usual. Non-essential personnel, females and children were calmly organizing in front of their assigned ships to be taken to the rendezvous point in the safe zone. This wasn't a full evacuation like Varsten had ordered, but a precautionary one.

With the lack of data from the probe, we had no proof

Sector 437 was next, but we weren't taking chances with non-military personnel.

Their relocation served two purposes, to remove the innocent from any chance of attack by the Hive's new weapon and to clear the flight bay of the non-military ships. We needed it available for incoming support squadrons, and quickly.

While there were some spots always left vacant, Prime Nial had ordered advanced strike and recon crafts to assist the Karter in finding the probe and then neutralizing it. We'd double the size of our fighter population and enhance our weapons, offense and striking capabilities. But they couldn't land until the other ships cleared out.

The transition was going smoothly, but I was still impatient. I was used to dealing with high-stress situations. The ship was battle-ready, my highest-ranking and most experienced leaders, some from engineering, some pilots, others from comms and navigation and infantry, surrounded me. The Atlans had sent their Commander, Warlord Wulf, a massive beast who'd seen even more war than I had. I had been waiting for him to go into mating fever for years now, but he always maintained control. I was starting to believe the bastard had some kind of superpower.

One of my most sincere hopes was that he would not go beast and rip my battleship to shreds before the new Hive weapon did.

Chloe and Ronan were present as well. The I.C. was well represented. Normally that thought wouldn't have bothered me.

Today? Today, I felt... different. On edge. It was all because of Erica. Reassurance of her safety on Prillon Prime eased my mind, but I still thought of her. No doubt she was furious with us for forcing transport on her. Her safety was top priority. I'd rather have her mad than dead.

And yet, the Personnel Commander, or PC, had asked after her, wished to liaise with her as to her orders. Erica, to the PC, was her boss and should be leading this relocation. She should be with the other civilian command team, consulting and adding her expertise.

I did not know exactly what my mate's talents were, as had spent more time fucking than talking, but after she left, I had taken some time to review her profile in the Interstellar Brides processing protocol files.

She was brilliant. A scientist who studied the stars and the universe. She had studied and earned advanced degrees and accolades on her home world. I did not know exactly what she did, or how her knowledge might be useful to my people, but I had spoken to Ronan briefly and we were in agreement.

First, we survive this battle, and then we dedicate every waking moment to learning about our female.

The smile in her photograph was filled with happiness and hope. She'd looked excited to face a new adventure. To venture out into space and meet her perfect mate. But, in this case, mates. And I knew I was not perfect.

Me?

Gods help her. I was not perfect, not in any way.

"Squadron 168 will arrive from Battlegroup Brekk in three hours," Captain Onar spoke. He'd been with me for years, former leader of the protection team at Transport Station Zenith. He was fierce and organized, his bronze hair and skin broken only by bright golden eyes. He held a tablet and was swiping across it as he spoke. "The fighter wing from the Zakar will arrive seventy minutes after that. We'll have five hundred fighters in the bay in the next twenty-seven hours, in addition to the three battleships coming from Prillon Prime."

"How long until most of the fighter reinforcements have

arrived?" I asked. The battleships were huge, with their own contingent of fighters. They would be at least a day behind the smaller, faster fighters that were being transported on massive transport pads to the nearest military bases and reassigned to the Battlegroup Karter.

"Six hours, as long as the bay is clear for them to land," Onar replied.

"Send us out there, Commander. We'll find them." Warlord Wulf stood still as a mountain, but I wasn't fooled. I'd seem him go beast on the battlefield, knew exactly the level of violence he was capable of.

"As soon as we find the fuckers, they're all yours, Warlord."

"Good." He pounded the fist of his left hand into his right palm, the boom so loud several warriors looked up from their work on the docks below.

Fucking Atlans.

I glanced at the PC, her cream-colored uniform a stark contrast to the battle gear worn by the rest of us. "We're on schedule, sir. All civilian vessels will be clear within the next two hours."

Turning, I looked to Chloe and Ronan. "What can the I.C. tell us?"

Everyone knew they were I.C., knew that some of their missions were top secret. I didn't care. The time for whispers and shadows was over.

"A plan to search for the weapon is in the works," Ronan commented. "I'll work with Onar to coordinate rest periods for our personnel as well as maintenance of the ships so we can send out advance squadrons. We'll mix the crafts so we have fighter ships side by side with scanner craft." He looked to the the Prillon captain, Onar, who nodded in agreement.

"Search groups will run 25/7," Chloe added. "Ronan and I

will be on different rotations along with two others from I.C. Central Command."

I nodded. "Good." My leaders were efficient and successful in their roles; that was why I had them. But they would be coordinating with I.C. as well as squadron leaders from multiple battlegroups. I had no specific physical task, nothing to do except organize, monitor and guide as needed. We weren't under fire. While I considered the entire battlegroup under possible imminent attack, there was no direct proof. I couldn't scramble or fight back when we didn't know *what* we were fighting.

I would not be deployed in the search groups. I would lead from here. It made me feel as if my hands were tied, in every facet of my life.

Imprisoned behind a comm table while I sent good warriors out to die. Tied to a female I didn't dare claim. Trapped in a sector of space I could not leave, head stretched out across a butcher's block, waiting for the Hive to strike.

"Commander," the PC said. She was Prillon, a collar about her neck indicating she was mated. I knew she had one child, although she was not being relocated with the other non-military personnel. I needed a civilian liaison here. If we had wounded, or lost any warriors, I needed a link to their mates and families close.

"Yes?"

"Will Lady Karter be joining the personnel in the safe zone? If I am to remain here to assist, they will need someone in charge. While I do have subordinates who can handle the task, I think everyone would be more comfortable with her presence."

What the PC said was true. As my mate, Erica became Lady Karter and was, while unwittingly and perhaps against her desires, in charge of all non-military personnel on the ship. That was thousands of individuals. And with those from the Varsten battlegroup mixed in, it was nearly double the usual count. While I'd been inside her body on several occasions, I didn't know much about her mind. I knew she was intelligent, but I had no idea why she'd volunteered to be a bride. Would she be a good leader? Would she even *want* to be?

"No, Lady Karter will not be going to the safe zone," I said. "I'm sure your team will be excellent support instead."

While the PC's eyes widened slightly, she only tipped her head in acknowledgement.

"I will go to the safe zone and take command of the civilians in the fleet."

The female voice from behind me had me spinning on my heel. I knew that voice, the soft timbre of contentment, the sharp bite of anger, even the breathy cry of pleasure.

Erica.

Ronan went immediately to her side, pulled her into his arms for a hug, then put his hands on her shoulders and pushed her back so he could look at her. "What are you doing here, mate?" His gaze ran over her. "Did something happen during transport? Are you hurt?"

It had only been thirty minutes since we'd sent her to Prillon Prime and the safety of Prime Nial's palace. He hadn't commed to say she hadn't arrived. Why the fuck was she here?

A thrill ran through me at seeing her, and yet, fear as well. She was not safe here.

"Oh, no. I met Lady Deston. We had a nice chat and she agreed that I should come back."

"Prime Nial allowed it?" I asked, stepping toward them. The others around us parted to let me by.

She shook her head, her long hair flowing down her back. I remembered it, just an hour ago, fisted in Ronan's hand as she sucked him off. Shit, I was getting hard.

She looked to me, tipped her chin up. "No, he was busy with *you*."

Oh, she was mad. I didn't have to be her mate to see it. Her body wasn't soft and supple as she was when aroused. Her muscles were tense, her mouth pressed into a thin line. Her eyes flared with anger.

"Jessica and I had a nice, little chat."

I glanced at Chloe who was smirking. Damned Earth females.

Erica lifted her hands, knocked Ronan's off her shoulders, then put her hands on her hips and glared at me like I was a naughty child.

Gods be damned, I hadn't seen that look on a female's face since I was a boy being scolded by my mother.

"I can't believe you sent me to Prillon Prime when I am now Lady Karter. Chloe said I was in charge of non-military personnel. I can't *do* that from a planet a trillion miles away."

"I need you to be safe, mate," I said.

She spun on her heel, the flowing brown dress I'd had rucked up around her waist as I fucked her, swirling about her long legs. She came over to me, actually pushed my chest. I didn't move, but she dared to shove me.

And that made my cock even harder.

This magnificent, feisty female was my mate.

"And yet there are *children* right over there." She pointed to deck three and the group that was boarding one of the cargo ships.

"They are leaving within ten minutes for a safe zone."

Her eyes narrowed. "A *safe* zone is *safe* enough for them but not *safe* for me?"

Oh fuck.

"You should go, love. We will worry over you otherwise," Ronan said.

That was obviously the wrong thing to say since her

mouth dropped open and she looked like Chloe had the time she made her mates sleep in the fighters' quarters for two nights.

"I am Lady Karter. I am here to assume my duties to lead my people. I do not need your permission, Lord High and Mighty. I will do what needs to be done, and you aren't going to stop me." Magnificent, perfect fucking female.

Leaning down, I whispered in her ear. "I can spank your ass, tie you up and carry you back to the transport pad."

She turned her head slightly so our lips almost touched. "You can try," she threatened. "If you do so, Kaed, then the testing was wrong, and I will not return. I will not be dictated to or coddled like a child. I am your mate, not a pair of boots to be tossed away when it's not convenient for you to have me around."

I arched a brow at her comment. Ronan came over so he stood beside us both. The group of commanders was probably still behind us, but I paid them no attention. I was focused solely on Erica as her words sank into my body. My soul. She was deadly serious. If I sent her away now, I would lose her forever.

My silence must have softened her heart, at least a little, for her tone was gentle when she spoke next, Ronan and I both leaning forward to catch every word.

"You disrespect me by not finding me worthy of my role. I do not wish to be reckless with my safety, but I will not walk away when my people need me, when *you* need me."

"Mate," Ronan said. "We would never disrespect you."

She turned and looked up at him. "But you have. You doubt our match."

I shook my head. "No. Never."

"Yet you think the testing didn't match you to someone strong enough to be at your side, to share your burdens, to take on the role of Lady Karter before your people. You expect me to walk among them, unclaimed, and explain to every curious eye why you have chosen *not* to claim me?"

I hadn't thought of it that way. Our lack of collar dishonored her and embarrassed her in front of my people. Her people.

"I trust you in your jobs. I trust that Ronan is careful when he goes out into the field. Chloe explained the I.C. to me and I know it is full of... peril. And you, being commander of an entire battlegroup, means you deal with bad stuff. You forget I arrived from Earth into the middle of a disaster. Why can't you trust me to handle myself in the same way?"

"We live under constant threat of attack," I told her.

She tilted her head to the side to look around me. "Chloe, where's your family?"

I heard the female's light footsteps as she approached. "Seth is boarding cargo ship #64 on deck one with the kids now. I showed the children how to make up constellations in the sky and it will keep them entertained on the journey. Seth will be in the safe zone with them while Dorian flies in one of the advance search groups."

Erica looked up at me again. "Her children have been on this ship all their young lives. If Chloe keeps them here, then don't belittle me by assuming me too weak to stay as well."

I clenched my hands into fists. "I will not have you harmed or exposed to the horrors of my job. Of Ronan's."

"Too late. I had warrior's blood on my hands the very first time you touched me, do you not remember?"

Ronan looked to me, and I could read his mind as if he were a comm message, a message I finally received. Erica wasn't the problem, I was. I was afraid of hurting her, losing her. Afraid the violence of my mind would frighten her away.

But if I did nothing, refused to take this chance, to trust her, I would lose her anyway.

"You will not remain on the Karter. You will go to the safe zone and lead. The PC will prep you before you leave and assign her top people to assist you."

The smile that lit her face was brilliant. In that moment, I knew I'd underestimated Erica. I'd thought, perhaps not even consciously, that she was weak. Incapable of life on the Karter. Of leading those under her care. I should have known better; from the first minutes in her company, she'd gone to tend to others.

She had a caring heart and a need to serve and I'd taken that from her.

"I won't go without a collar."

Ronan smirked and I crossed my hands over my chest.

"Now you give the orders?" I asked.

"I will not be Lady Karter in all ways but one."

Yes, it appeared that in this mating, she would indeed be giving the orders.

And I'd be blessed by the gods themselves to follow them.

"Are you sure, Erica? You might want to be involved with the evacuation, but that is different than knowing what I feel. What I sense. The burden is great."

She sighed. "Again, you underestimate me. Perhaps you are forgetting that you will know what I feel, what I sense. Perhaps that will lift you up, not take me down."

"Ah, mate," Ronan said, cupping her cheek with his hand. "Give him hell, Erica. Make him beg." He kissed her on the lips, hard. Fast. "I want to see it, at least once in this lifetime."

Erica smiled up into his eyes and wrapped her arms around him. They had both made up their minds, as had I. I would trust in the matching protocol, trust in my family, in the female who held my heart in the palm of her small, human hand.

"Very well," I said. I had fought this long and hard, but knew it wasn't something I could win. She would soon learn the burden I carried, and I hoped the testing was correct and she could handle it. I turned to the PC. "Send someone to fetch my collars from my office."

She turned and fled with haste.

"Kaed, you need to go with her," Ronan said.

I frowned. "To the safe zone?"

He nodded. "One mate should remain with her, in safety. Need I remind you of the main reason for a second in Prillon mating?"

"No," I snapped.

"Remind me," Erica said.

"A mate is cherished, loved, protected and possessed by her two mates. Because Prillons are mostly fighters, death is a strong possibility. Having a second means a mate will never be without a male. For love, for children, for their future." Ronan kissed her forehead. Damn him for being the gentle one. I felt like an Atlan beast in comparison.

"I must lead one of the advanced groups so the Hive doesn't win this fight. It will reassure me to know he is with you. That if I die, you will not be alone."

"Ronan," she whispered, then nodded.

I wanted to argue with him, but I sighed instead. I didn't want to fight anymore. I was jaded, angry, stressed. Frustrated. I was at my breaking point at the thought of losing her. Was that why I'd been matched? Was the testing that accurate to know exactly when I needed a mate to take care of instead of leading others into battle?

Was my new role not only commander, but Erica's mate? Her personal protector?

"You are the commanders' mate, Erica. One will lead while the other remains at your side, protecting you," Ronan added.

The PC returned with the familiar box that held my collars. I opened it, took the three out and handed the empty box back to the PC. She smiled as she took it from me, then stepped back.

"I will not claim you in the usual Prillon custom, mate," I said.

"But—"

I put a finger over her lips. "It involves stripping you naked and fucking you. In a traditional claiming, I would be deep in your pussy and Ronan in your ass as witnesses observe and chant."

She flushed a bright pink at the words. I took my finger away. "Oh."

"Yes, oh."

"I have made one concession already by allowing Ronan to have your pussy in equal measure. I will not allow anyone to see you as your mates do, your body is for the two of us only. The sight of you coming, the sound of it, belongs to us."

"We'd be sharing your body here. Now. Do you wish for your claiming to occur in the landing bay of a battleship?" Ronan asked.

She swallowed. "Do we have to do that, in front of everyone? I admit, I'm not really into exhibitionism."

I shook my head. "No, we will modify the ceremony."

Stepping back, I faced the team of group leaders. "As you've probably overheard, Lady Karter and I will be going with the cargo ships to coordinate the battle from the safe zone. I will lead the fighters and she will lead the civilian teams to care for your mates and families. Since we are short on time, you shall witness our modified claiming."

They moved silently and quickly into a semi-circle around myself, Ronan and Erica. I handed two of the collars to Ronan and I lifted one to my neck, wrapped it around and closed it. While I couldn't see, I assumed the color went from black to brown, my family color: the Karter family's, for hundreds of years.

I took one back from him as he affixed his about his own neck. As his collar changed color, I felt the connection, the power of the bond the collars gave us. I felt his emotions, the pride in this moment, his contentment with Erica. The desire, the love, the need. I also felt the pressure of his job, of the Hive, of what was to come, but I pushed all of that down, just as I did with my own thoughts not related to this moment.

I wouldn't ruin this moment for Erica by focusing on dark thoughts. She would learn the weight of our connection soon enough. Right now, in this moment, I wanted her to feel all the need I had for her. Lust. Love. Desire. Trust. Pride. Everything I felt when I looked at her was tangled up into a knot so tight I had no hope of unraveling it.

I turned, looked to the captains and commanders who surrounded us, the leadership team that would see us through the coming battle, and nodded.

They began to chant, softly, yet in direct accord with the mating ritual. Their voices rang out strong and clear, and soon every warrior in the landing bay, as well as the civilians had joined the chant. To bear witness to a claiming was to be honored, chosen as a trusted guardian and friend to the mated trio. Including everyone here felt... right. She belonged to them as well. Their Lady.

Erica's eyes widened as the volume rose, but she tilted her chin up, ready. Ronan placed his hands upon her shoulders, turned her to face me directly, then collected her long hair in his hand, held it aloft.

With steady hands, I put the collar about her neck. I was aware that this moment was life altering. Forever. I cleared my throat and looked into her eyes. "Do you accept my claim, mate? Do you give yourself to me and my second freely, or do you wish to choose another primary male?"

"I accept your claim, warriors." I didn't know how she

knew the words to say, but she did. I took them into me. Felt them. Felt Ronan savor them.

"Then we claim you in the rite of naming. You are mine and I shall kill any other warrior who dares to touch you."

The group of witnesses—no, fuck that—the entire battle-group said in unison, "May the gods witness and protect you."

The sound reverberated off the walls, came from every comm station and communicator. Somewhere along the way, the scene had been broadcast to the entire ship.

One glance at Chloe Phan and I knew who to blame... and who to thank. Not one crew member or civilian in this battlegroup would doubt my devotion to Erica now.

I closed the collar about her neck, the bond complete. Her collar changed from deep black to warm brown. She gasped, her fingers going to the collar.

I felt her. Felt every part of her being. And now she felt me. Knew the truth about me, how weak I truly was, how terrified of losing the battleship, of leading my people into death. She knew exactly how badly I needed her, and how unworthy I was of her love.

There was no going back. She knew it all.

CHAPTER 12

Erica, Battleship Karter, Shuttle Dock 4

Kaed's hand was in mine as he led me toward the shuttle that would take us to safety. A group of civilians and non-essential personnel would be joining us. His touch was different, his bearing, even the way he walked. He was in commander mode, the part of him his people needed right now. I understood the difference.

And now I understood part of the reason my mate had tried to deny me his collar.

He had a stone-cold exterior with molten lava on the inside. Makaed Karter was a silent storm, his emotions more powerful than I ever could have imagined. Pride in his people. Honor and humility at being trusted to lead them. Fear that he would let them down. Self-loathing for what he perceived as his own weakness, at his need for something to have for himself.

His need for me.

Ronan approached and I let Kaed go long enough to wrap

my arms around my second and kiss him. "Come back to me, Ronan."

"I will, mate." The sincerity of his vow, and the depth of his commitment to me came through the collars like a blast of cool wind, wiping Kaed's need from my mind—and his.

I kissed my second, because I could, because I wanted to let loose my love for these two stubborn warriors at least once before he marched—or flew off—into danger. They both felt it, as they were meant to. Their combined desire and love blasted through me until I could barely stand.

God, if this was what they felt like in the middle of chaos in a shuttle bay, what was it going to be like when we were alone? Naked?

Ronan groaned and broke the kiss. "Mate, you give me another reason to return." He smiled.

I smiled back. "What's that?"

"I will have you naked and screaming my name, female."

He'd known my thoughts. The collars!

I stepped back, my hand slipping from his slowly until just our fingers touched. Then, nothing. "I'm going to hold you to that promise, mate."

Kaed's arm wrapped around my waist and he pulled my back to his chest. Mine again. For now. "Return to us Ronan. We'll be waiting."

Ronan gave a small salute and walked toward what looked like a super-cool black fighter jet. Except there were no jet engines. And it was a triangle. And black.

Nope. Didn't really look like a jet at all, except for the guns and missiles mounted under the wings. Rows and rows of similar fighter ships, all with pilots scrambling to get inside and go hunting for the Hive were waiting to take flight.

"Shall we, Erica? We need to evacuate with the others."

I nodded and allowed my mate to lead me toward the

shuttlecraft as another fighter lifted off the floor of the launch bay and shot off into space like a silent rocket. I stared at the fighter as it grew smaller and smaller, until it was the size of a star. That pilot was flying toward Chloe's skateboard constellation.

The thought made me smile.

And stop dead in my tracks. "Kaed?"

"Yes, mate? What's wrong?"

For a split second, I wondered how he knew I was upset, but then I realized that for the first time since we'd placed the collars around our necks, my emotion was stronger than his. He *sensed* it. "There is something out there."

Ronan appeared two steps ahead of us, as if I'd summoned him. "What's wrong? I felt you, Erica. What is it?"

Kaed looked out the giant view of the stars offered by the invisible energy barrier that kept the air inside the flight deck, but allowed the fighters and cargo shuttles to pass through. How it worked, I had no idea. "I don't see anything. What do you see? Where is it?"

I pulled Kaed down so that his face was next to mine, our cheeks touching, and raised my hand to point at the skateboard constellation Chloe had invented—and its *three* large wheels. "There. Do you see the line of stars that looks like a skateboard?"

"A what?" Ronan had his cheek pressed to the opposite side of my face, looking.

"A skateboard."

They both drew a blank, and I saw Chloe walking toward a fighter. "Chloe!" I screamed her name at the top of my lungs, but she didn't hear me. My mates jumped back, startled by my shout.

I turned to my mates. "I need Chloe. Or we need to go somewhere you have star maps and a telescope."

Both of my mates bellowed for Commander Phan and she heard them, loud and clear. No doubt, so did half of the ship.

She jogged over, a frown on her face. "What is it?"

All three of them looked at me. I turned Chloe around and pointed over her shoulder. "You see the skateboard?"

"Yes." She'd found it, named it, claimed it. I was relieved that she remembered. Not everyone was as star crazy as I was.

"How many wheels does it have?"

"Two—oh, shit. Three. Something's out there. Something big." She whirled and tapped the button for her comms. "I.C.C. – this is Commander Chloe Phan. The Karter has visual on a Hive attack vessel. Preparing to engage. Download all starboard visual data surrounding Beta Cluster 7-9-5-5. Analyze for anomalies."

When she was done, I stared in shock. "Beta Cluster 7-9-5-5?"

She grinned. "Skateboard is a cooler name, but the Prillons don't get really creative, nor do they know what a skateboard is."

My mates were both transfixed, staring out into the stars.

"Fuck. I see it," Ronan said, turning to look at me. "It has to be huge. How did you know it was there? No one has seen it until now."

I shrugged. "On Earth I was an astronomer. It's what I do, I watch the stars. They're familiar to me, until they aren't. Like this thing in Beta Cluster... whatever."

His shocked fascination blended with Kaed's rage at the immediate threat to his people. It was his turn to tap his comm. "Bard, this is Karter. Hive sighted starboard. Beta Cluster 7-9-5-5. Attack imminent. Sound the alarms. I want everyone off this ship. Evasive maneuvers. Reroute the evacuation vessels to new coordinates. Send the fighters out to intercept and buy them some time."

"Yes, Commander. Confirmed. We have a visual."

"Transmit visuals to I.C. and Prillon Prime. Broadcast to the incoming battlegroups. They need to know what to look for. This might not be the only one."

"Copy, Commander. Battle alarms in three."

The link went dead, but two seconds later the entire ship vibrated as an alarm rumbled through the air. Not a high-pitched screech, like I'd been expecting. More like what I imagined an Atlan beast might sound like when it roared on the battlefield.

Ronan grabbed me, kissed me hard. "We have much to learn about you." He took off running toward his fighter. I made sure to fill my entire being with love so he would feel it and come back to me.

Chloe gave me a quick hug. "Just like finding the Death Star in *Star Wars,* huh?"

I thought of the movie and the huge evil space ship that had blown Alderaan to bits.

I couldn't answer because she was already halfway to her own ship. She was going to be in the heart of this battle, and her mates were going to have to deal with that, just like I had to watch Ronan walk away.

Next to me, Commander Karter was a pool of calm, the layer of ice he'd placed over his emotions calming me as well. "You amaze me constantly, mate. Come. It's time to get you off this ship."

I didn't argue, not one bit.

onan, Stealth Fighter Prototype HS-7, I.C. Defense Special Issue

. . .

I was halfway to the Hive weapon ship, flying solo. I didn't have time to wait for the rest of the fighter teams to catch up. I needed to be up close and personal, gathering intel on that stealth ship and its weapons before the actual fighting started. "Going ghost, Karter. I'm going to disappear from your sensors in three... two... one... ghost."

"Confirmed. No hits on sensors. Stealth mode engaged. Good luck, Commander."

I was going to need all the luck I could get.

Fifteen silent minutes later, I flew directly at the ship that I assumed was responsible for the destruction of the Hyrad Battlegroup. Nine thousand lives lost. The Varsten. Thirty of the toughest warriors I knew, friends, dead, along with one of the most respected battle commanders in the fleet.

And now the Hive was hunting the Karter and her crew. My mate and my new people. I hadn't had a home for five long years. Longer, if I was being honest with myself. Erica and Kaed were my family now. Even so far from them, I could still feel the fierce pride and deep love Karter had for Erica as his mate, and for me—as his best friend and brother in all but blood. Erica's pure, fearless love had poured through me like fire washing away the cobwebs and filth from my soul. I'd never felt anything so powerful, so pure. So fucking courageous. Love like that was dangerous. All in. Live or die. Dangerous.

Her courage shamed me as nothing else ever had or would. She dared to love us, despite our flaws, and we'd been stupid enough to think we were the strong ones in this mating.

We were weaklings compared to her fierce spirit. I'd do anything to protect her. Anything at all. Like flying right for a Hive super-weapon.

Reaching for the controls, I deployed the decoy communication buoys behind me. Seven of them. They would bounce the quantum communication signal directly from my ship, around the Hive sensors and back to the battleship. Unless the Hive were scanning every single light frequency, they wouldn't be able to hear or see me.

Being in the I.C. had a few perks, and one of them was this ship. Fitted with the latest in stealth technology, I could go anywhere undetected.

It worked. I knew it worked, because we'd stolen the technology from the enemy. My fighter ship had been reverse engineered from Hive technology we'd recovered on the Colony moon.

Another reason I wanted to meet the human female, Gwen, and thank her personally for leaving behind the garbage for us to find.

When the comm pinged that the relays were all in place, I opened the data link to the Karter. "Battleship Karter, this is Commander Wothar. Do you copy?"

"Confirmed. Go ahead, Commander."

"Activating visual. Please confirm."

I waited as the data from my ship's camera systems were transmitted back to the battleship, two, maybe three seconds to get through all of the light relays. "Confirmed visuals. We are recording. Proceed."

"Copy. I'm going in."

Pulling back on the throttle, I approached slowly, drifting toward the massive structure. The Hive ship was huge, easily five times the size of Battleship Karter. I'd never seen anything like it, and I'd seen too fucking much in this war.

"Battleship Karter, this is Commander Wothar. Are you getting this?"

"Affirmative, Commander. Rerouting to I.C. Command and Prillon Prime, as instructed."

"Good. Stay with me as long as you can." That was an

order for them to record and rebroadcast everything I did, everything I saw and everything I said—until I said nothing at all. In which case, I'd be dead, but the information I gathered would not die with me.

"Understood, sir."

I killed the chatter and flew closer to the giant ship. The shape of a massive rod at least half a mile wide and a mile long, the ship spun around like a floating bullet revolving through space toward its target. The sides were rough, meant to look like an asteroid or stray rock rotating on its axis. Just another space rock, except the front was tipped into the shape of a five-pointed star that pointed directly at Battleship Karter and her crew.

Over my dead body.

The weapons array was massive, nearly as large as Battleship Karter all by itself. "Holy fuck. This thing is huge. I'm getting in there."

"Back off, Ronan. You're too close. Wait for the rest of us. We're two minutes behind you." Commander Phan's voice filled my small cockpit, but I didn't take orders from her. Or Karter. The only one who could order me off this run was Prime Nial himself, and he was the one who had ordered me into the mouth of the beast in the first place. I had every intention of making sure whatever this was, no other battlegroup or planet would be caught unaware. Not again.

Too many were dead now because of this Hive ship.

"Stay back, Chloe. They can't see me. Fifty fighters flying right at them, and they'll launch a response."

"Damn it, Ronan." Chloe cursed at me, but I was right, and she knew it. "I can't let them fly right past us. The Karter's back there. We have orders to intercept."

"I know." My ship slipped into the cave-like mouth of the weapon's star shaped opening, and I peered at the towering crystalline formations within, circled slowly, making sure I got a clear vid of every inch of the new weapon. "Draw them off, if you have too. But stay away from the bow. I'm in stealth mode, but I don't need company."

"Copy that. All fighters on me. Battle formation. Keep it tight. We'll come in on their six. We'll try to keep them away from you, Ronan. Do what you can. Yell if you need help."

"Confirmed." I continued my report. *Their six* meant the rear of the ship. It was Earth slang, but everyone in the fleet had picked it up quickly, once the humans started showing up in fight squadrons. They were good pilots. Small. Fast. Coordinated. And fearless. Human ReCon teams had saved thousands of warriors, breaking into Hive-controlled vessels and dragging our people out.

And now, another female, *my mate*, might be the sole reason we destroyed the Hive's newest weapon. Erica Roberts might just save us all with her brilliant mind. Had she been matched because of her knowledge of the stars? Was she matched to save us all in this moment? I doubted I would ever know that answer.

Pride swelled in me nonetheless, but I had a job to do. "Star formations, five points, weapons' cluster is located inside the bow of the ship. Looks like magnetic coils the size of shuttle craft wrapped around the base of each crystal array." I flew in deeper, took a couple shots at one of the arrays with my ion blasters as the sounds of voices shouting, shots fired and the general chaos of battle filled my small cockpit with noise. I turned off incoming transmissions, kept the data flow out open wide. I could not afford distractions.

The ion blasts my ship fired bounced off the arrays like insults off Kaed's back. "Close range ion blaster fire is ineffective. Switching to rail guns."

Rail guns were old tech. Centuries old, but the Fleet had continued to use them. Sometimes the best weapons were tried and true.

I fired. Flew close. Watched. Waited.

Not a scratch, and I had to scramble to make the turn before I crashed into the side of the Hive ship. It was like flying inside a cave full of massive, indestructible stalagmites towering up from their bases to point out into the stars. At us.

At life.

At my mate.

Fuck.

I turned my comms back on to monitor the battle. It sounded like hell out there. Our fighters were being swarmed.

"Ronan! Whatever you're doing, make it fast. It's like you just kicked the beehive and they're pissed, pouring out like water. We're outnumbered and overrun. We can't hold our position much longer."

As Phan spoke, three drone fighters appeared above me, their scanners on, looking for the threat. I went dark, melting into the side of their ship beneath one of the huge coils. I was still in stealth mode, which meant they wouldn't see my ship unless they looked with their own eyes. Not likely. Like all the warriors in this war, we relied too heavily on our sensors and gear, and not enough on our own instincts. Our sight. Our senses.

But then, the Hive were assimilated, part of a large, collective group-think. Did they still have instincts?

"Karter, this is Commander Wothar." I spoke quietly, even though I didn't need to. Instinct.

"Go ahead, Commander." The voice in my ear was clipped, no doubt the warrior was stressed and heavily engaged in orchestrating the fight going on just out of my sight.

"Ion blasters and rail guns were ineffective. Do you have

electromagnetic, computational and radioactive data readings on the target?"

"Affirmative. We've got it all. Transmission to Prillon Prime is nearing completion. Transmission to I.C. will be complete in the next five minutes." Intelligence Core Command was significantly farther from my present location than Prillon Prime.

"Make sure you send data to the rest of the fleet commanders. Do it now. I don't want this data delayed. The Hive might have another ship like this out there, ready to attack the Fleet." If I.C. had something to say to me about this later, I'd deal with their wrath. The fleet commanders had a right to know what we were up against out here.

"Yes, sir. Working on that now."

Relieved the comm officer had not argued, I sagged in the pilot's seat, suddenly exhausted. No more secrets. No more surprise attacks by the Hive. Every fleet commander out there would know what to look for. My mate would be protected, and so would the rest of the fleet.

"You need anything else, Commander Karter?" I was speaking to Kaed now, and I trusted him to know what I was really asking. I might die out here, and I needed his blessing. I needed to know that he understood my choice. "I'm going to make sure this fucking ship can't hurt our mate or anyone else."

I counted to twenty as I waited for his answer. "Ronan, do what you have to do."

He knew what I was thinking. Nothing was working. My standard weapons were not causing any damage to the Hive structure. But I had an idea. A crazy as fuck idea, but it was all I had. With reinforcements too far away to help now, the Karter would not survive until their arrival, not with this weapon operational. And without the battleship to protect them, the smaller vessels would be hunted down and picked off one by one. Captured. Assimilated into the Hive's army. Unless I could destroy this weapon.

The prototype fighter I flew carried enough ordnance to destroy a small planet. All I had to do was figure out a way to get clear of the blast. And if I couldn't? Well, the Hive ship still needed to be destroyed.

Nothing else mattered.

The Hive ships above me scanned once more before moving on.

No eyes. No ears. Just sensors.

"Commander Phan, retreat. Get your fighters out of there."

"Understood. Battle squad leaders, you heard the commander. Clear out and head for the Karter." Chloe sounded breathless, as if she'd been running a marathon, not flying a fighter. But I understood the physical demands of fighting in space. She was tough.

"Negative. Lead them away from home. Evacuations are not yet complete." I gave the order, not Commander Karter. It had only been a short time. There was no way all the civilians were off the battleship.

"Lead them away, Commander Phan. I'll have something special waiting for them."

"Copy that, sir." Chloe sounded excited, and I smiled as dozens of Coalition fighters zipped over my head in a flash of silver light, almost too fast to see with the naked eye.

I waited in silence, expecting to see Hive fighters in pursuit, but none followed.

"They're letting us go. No pursuit, Karter. I repeat, no pursuit." Chloe sounded confused. I was too, until my ship rumbled beneath me.

"They are activating their primary weapon," I reported the news with nausea rolling in my gut. Of course, the Hive would pull back their ships. They were about to blow the entire battlegroup to pieces.

"Altering course," Chloe said.

"No." I unbuckled from my seat and slid to the back of the small ship, to the storage racks. This ship wasn't big, but every last inch was loaded with weapons and explosives. "Stay clear of the blast zone. Keep the fighters clear."

She heard me. Thank the gods. "How long?"

I checked the timer on my wrist. "Three minutes. Maybe four." I put one foot into the leg of the blast suit and pulled. The other. Zipper. Mask. Gloves.

If I could get out of range of the initial burn of the explosion, I might make it. "When it's over, come looking for the unconscious idiot floating in a space suit." I had no doubt, even if I survived the explosion, it would probably knock me out, at least for a few minutes. I'd have one hell of a headache for a while, but hopefully, I'd live. With Erica in my life, I very much wanted to do just that.

Chloe laughed, which made me grin. "Idiot hunting is one of my favorite games."

"With mates like Seth and Dorian, that's what I figured."

"Watch your mouth, Warrior." That was Dorian. I figured he'd be out here. He was one of the best pilots in the fleet. "That's my mate you're insulting."

I chuckled and activated the timed detonation device on the first set of explosives. The I.C. didn't like to share. And we'd not only copied the Hive tech we scavenged from the Colony, but advanced it. The self-destruct setting on my ship, once activated, was irreversible. "I would never insult your perfect female, only her choice in mates." Activated number two. "Must have been slim pickings on the Karter when she arrived."

That was, of course, a blatant lie. Chloe Phan of Earth had been matched through the Interstellar Brides Processing protocols. Which meant that Seth Mills, and his choice of second in Dorian, were ninety-nine percent guaranteed to make her happy.

Just like the matching protocols had given Erica to Kaed, and to me.

I thought of my family, back on the Karter, or the freighter where they should be right now. Safe. Out of the line of fire.

How did Seth Mills tolerate having both Chloe and Dorian out on these missions? They had not one child, but two, Dara and Christopher. Two beautiful, perfect children. Yet two of their parents were out here, in battle, risking their lives.

Ordnance set to go off in ninety seconds, I activated the self-destruct countdown and opened the escape hatch on the roof my fighter. I had to crawl out instead of float, the Hive ship's rotation creating a weak artificial gravity that was just strong enough to hold me down.

Fuck. I'd planned on giving a good kick and floating out of here.

"Eighty seconds. Repeat, eight-zero seconds."

"Copy that, Commander. Get out of there."

I jump-floated down from the roof of the fighter to the surface of the cavern-like structure. Around me, the emptiness of space should have felt like... nothing. Instead, my entire body buzzed, as if I were being shaken from the inside out as the coils and crystal array powered up all around me.

I glanced down at my ship as I scrambled on all fours up the curved side of the star-shaped basin. At least she was recording everything and sending it back.

I glanced at the heads-up display inside my visor. We would be collecting data for sixty-two more seconds.

Was the Hive ship going to fire before the bombs could take her out?

Fuck. Fuck. Fuck.

"Clear the Karter. I'm not sure the explosion will take out the weapon in time."

Kaed's voice came on over my comm. "You've done what you can. Now get the fuck out of there, Ronan. That's an order."

I could argue, but I wasn't going to waste energy when I needed to get out of this crater and into open space. It was the only chance I had. I couldn't change the countdown from here. That was one of the fail-safes built into the system. Self-destruction assured. Once activated, there was no turning it off – from inside or out.

CHAPTER 13

Erica, Freight Craft BK5-8, Battlegroup Karter

The people were scared. So was I. But we were all putting on a brave face and smiling for the handful of children running around, chasing each other in circles, as if the ride on this freighter was one great big adventure. I even heard one small Prillon boy whoop for joy about getting out of an exam that afternoon in school.

Seemed kids were kids everywhere. I could remember being excited about a snow day now and again. No school. Snow forts and snowball fights followed by hot chocolate and a lesson from my dad on how snow crystals formed.

We'd placed water on glass slides and put then in the freezer. When my dad placed them under his microscope and beckoned me over, a scientist had been born.

I'd been seven years old, and I could remember that moment, and his big, warm hand on my back like it was yesterday.

I held onto that memory as I walked among the scared

mothers and medics, their children and the elders who'd chosen to spend the remainder of their lives out here in space, training the younger males or serving as mentors and counselors. They were all here, all smiling their tense smiles for the same reason I was.

Commander Makaed Karter.

They believed in him, and so did I.

"Lady Karter! Lady Karter! Come play with us!" One of the young ladies beckoned to me from where she was seated near an overturned crate. The boys were being boys, rough-housing and chasing each other in a game that appeared to me a mixture between soccer and wrestling. I suspected the wrestling was not expressly part of the game.

"Please, Lady Karter. Do join us." One of the ladies' mothers smiled at me. If I had to guess, I'd say she was an Atlan, because she was at least a foot taller than me and had even more curves.

For a minute, I wondered why I hadn't been matched to an Atlan, they did seem to enjoy ladies with a few extra curves. But then I saw the collar around her neck and realized she was Atlan, but her mates were Prillon warriors, just like mine.

Duh. I'd never thought of that. Everyone went everywhere. Atlan women for Prillon warriors. Prillon women for Atlans. I knew there were other races as well, but I wondered if an Atlan woman was ever mated to a human. Since Chloe had told me she was actually mated to Seth Mills, a human, I'd begun to wonder about that as well.

So much to learn. I hoped I would have time to study everything. But for now, I could sit and smile and play cards with these beautiful young ladies.

"Of course. I'd be honored." I walked to the crate and one of them found a makeshift chair for me so I would not have to sit on the cold freighter's floor. I took a seat and looked around with a smile seeing a beautiful little girl sitting on one of the older girl's laps. The teenager was Prillon, with copper-colored hair and eyes and gorgeous golden skin just like Ronan's.

She smiled at me, as did the toddler. She was so young and small and perfectly content sitting on the young lady's lap. So innocent.

I would not be the one to frighten any of them.

"You're going to have to teach me how to play this game. I've never played it before." I looked at the cards on the table, shocked to discover they looked exactly like a standard deck of playing cards from Earth. Shaking off the déjà vu, I turned and looked at each of the women in turn. There were six, and they were all smiling like they'd just won the lottery. "And please, tell me your names. It will take me a while to learn them all, so please forgive me if I don't remember right away."

The girl holding the child grinned. "I'm Kamara. This is Commander Chloe's daughter, Dara."

I held out my hand. "I'm Erica. Pleasure to meet you."

Kamara beamed proudly as I shook her hand, but it didn't last long, little Dara shoved her hand between ours until it was a three-way shake. Impatient and bold. Just like her mother.

"Dara, where are your manners, love. Wait your turn." That warm, doting voice came out of the shadows, and I turned to find a human man standing there with a golden, Prillon mating collar around his neck.

"You must be Captain Seth Mills," I said, smiling to see whom I guessed was his son, Christopher, on his hip as the man stepped forward and nodded.

The little boy had black hair, just like his sister. But instead of Dara's bright green eyes, his were golden, as was his skin. He was very obviously half Prillon, and I assumed that as the primary male, Seth had claimed his rights to have the first child, giving Dorian the second.

I thought of the Chloe I knew allowing that and decided I had to be wrong. I just couldn't see her following with that custom.

These children were gifts of Fate, and I wanted some of my own. "Your children are beautiful."

His smile was genuine and the love in his eyes was, too. But I was confused. "Shouldn't you be—you know—somewhere else?" I didn't want to scare the children, but I was curious. "You're a captain, right? Why did Commander Karter put you back here with the children?"

Seth's smile faded, but it was replaced with understanding, not anger. "I run ReCon. I'm not a pilot. Dorian and Chloe are both excellent pilots. I'm best at close quarters fighting."

He twisted his torso so I could see the stash of weapons he had attached to his lower back and thighs, and I understood. If things went badly, he was doing double duty: staying with his kids so Chloe and Dorian could fly, and serving as last line of defense of the mates and children. He'd die to protect them, especially with his own little ones here. But I understood the honor and trust my mate and the other mated males had placed in him to protect what was most precious to them.

"I see." And I did. I made sure to add an extra nod of acknowledgment in his direction. I understood more than he was saying.

Dara crawled down from the Kamara's lap as she was dealing all of us four cards. There were two more women at the table now. As Lady Karter, I was, it seemed, something of a celebrity.

Dara pulled on her father's pant leg and he grinned down, scooping her up into his opposite arm, and out of her brother's reach. His chubby little fingers were already reaching for her long, black hair. "Daddy smashes them. Don't you, Daddy?" Her voice was all toddler, but I understood every word and peace filled me as she nuzzled her little head under his chin.

"That's right, baby girl. Your daddy is more a smash and grab kind of guy." He kissed the top of her head and looked back to me. "I'm not into lining up in formation and getting shot at."

Kamara pushed four cards across the makeshift table and smiled. "This is Commander Phan's favorite Earth game."

I picked up my four cards and looked them over. Pretty standard crap hand. One jack of spades, a seven of diamonds, three of hearts, and a joker. "Okay. What is it?"

"Do you know how to play Go Fish?"

I nearly burst out laughing, until I saw that Kamara was very, very serious. "Yes, I do, as a matter of fact. That's Commander Phan's favorite game?"

"Yes. With joker's wild." Her smile faded for a moment. "Do you know what a joker is?"

I laughed out loud, the sound happy and free and empty of tension. Many eyes were pulled in our direction, and I let them look. I was Lady Karter and these were my people. And right now, they desperately needed to laugh.

Three games later, Dara was on *my* lap, Christopher on Kamara's and we had a mix of boys and girls playing the game. I'd also learned that Chloe's idea of going fishing was not exactly standard practice on Earth.

If one had to "Go Fish" they had to do a physical feat of strength, or grace, before they were allowed to draw another card. Which meant push-ups, sit-ups, running in place, or showing off a magic trick or dance move. Most of the girls danced. Most of the boys showed off, and even Christopher, who could toddle around on unsteady feet, decided to get in on the action.

That set everyone to laughing, adults and kids alike, and the little hero was a total ham, bouncing up and down on his chunky baby thighs and swinging his arms like he was at a dance party.

OMG, I wanted one.

I was swirling with Dara in my arms when Kaed's pain hit me. Hard.

Kissing Dara on the cheek, I kept up the swaying and whirling as I danced Dara back over to her father. One look in my eyes and he knew something was up even before I spoke. "I need to find Commander Karter and get an update."

He nodded and took his daughter from me, kissing her on her belly until she squealed and kicked and begged to be put down. When he placed her on her feet, she raced back to where her baby brother was still the center of attention, took his hands and they danced together. Family.

I glanced around at the people smiling and loving each other. This was family. My family. All of them. But Kaed needed me. I could feel him through the collar. Suffering.

"Do you know where he is? I don't want to wander all over the ship."

Seth turned to Kamara. "Can you keep an eye on Dara and Christopher for me? I need to show Lady Karter the way to the command deck. I'll be right back."

The girl's shoulders got a little straighter and she puffed up with pride. "Of course, Captain. I'd be honored."

I touched her shoulder in thanks as we walked past, absolutely certain Chloe's little ones would be well looked after in Seth's absence. Once the door closed behind us and we were alone in the corridor, I turned to Seth.

"How do you do it? Let them both go fight at the same

time?" I thought of both Kaed and Ronan being out there, fighting, and shuddered. "I'm not sure I could stand it."

His smile was all too human and I instantly liked him. No wonder Chloe loved this man. "You're doing it right now. They're both in battle, Lady Karter. Just because the commander is on this ship doesn't mean he's not fighting. Fighting is easy. You fight. You live or you die. It's harder being the one left behind."

He walked me to the control room where my mate was surrounded by buzzing warriors. The scene was controlled chaos, every screen, and there were a lot of them, moving. Ships. Grids. Missile projections. Everyone seemed to be talking at once, but to the warriors out there, in space, rather than to each other. And yet, I sensed that every single one of them knew exactly what was happening.

Kaed was bent over, his head down as he looked at something on a display in front of him. He looked fierce. Strong. So confident and disciplined. Only I could sense his pain, his frustration, his desperate need to lift his head and rage.

Everyone else in the room seemed calm, well, as calm as could be expected. His pain was personal and ran deep. Which meant only one thing... Ronan. Something had happened to Ronan.

He was camouflaged. The commander in action, and I began to understand why he had hesitated to trust me with this—connection. It made him vulnerable. What I did next could crack through that armor. Make him weak.

He sensed my presence, turning to face me. His face was as cold and emotionless as granite. I understood, burying my own pain at the idea that Ronan was hurt, or worse, gone forever. I buried my anxiety, frustration and worry and replaced the emotions with calm. Kaed needed me to be strong. I would not be the weakling he'd feared I would be if faced with this situation. Summoning my memories, I called upon my hours and hours of staring out at the sky, up at the planets and stars, with complete serenity. In those moments, I'd felt like I was part of something much, much bigger than myself.

And with that surety came peace. I felt it now, and I focused on that feeling, willing Kaed to take what he needed from me.

"Are you well, mate?" he asked, the entire bridge crew froze as if holding their collective breath for my answer.

I held his gaze and nodded. "I am well, Commander. I just wanted to update you that all of the passengers are comfortable and well taken care of."

"Excellent." He inclined his head and I felt his gratitude pour into me, his relief that I was not going to ask him what was tearing him up inside. Not now.

"Do you all need anything here?" Kaed's emotional turmoil calmed and I filled my heart with love. Peace. Acceptance. This was the life I had chosen. He was the mate I had chosen. No matter what happened next, whether we all died in the next hour, or lived another hundred years, I did not regret that choice.

The support crew declined, ignoring me, returning their attention to the battle. As they should. Seth titled his head and motioned for me to join him as he headed back to check on his children.

"Very well." I turned, leaving my mate with a smile I hoped would make him understand. But dealing with the battle, the crew and the threat to Ronan was an emotional struggle I could not fight for him.

The door slid closed behind us and I turned on my heel just as Seth's hand came down on my shoulder, a very human move. No Prillon would touch me this way, but I was grateful for the human comfort. "You did well in there."

"Thanks."

He stopped me in my tracks and gently turned me to face him. "Erica. Listen to me. You did well."

I pasted on a smile and straightened my shoulders. "Yeah? Well, someone very smart told me that being left behind was harder than fighting."

"I did." He squeezed gently and let me go. "And now you know."

"Now, I know." And I did. Ronan was fighting. Kaed was fighting. I had to be strong, trust them and do my job. I was Lady freaking Karter, these were my people, my mates, and my ship.

CHAPTER 14

Ronan

The countdown in the corner of my visor fed adrenaline to every muscle in my body as I jumped and clawed my way up out of the crater of the Hive ship. Twenty-seven seconds until I was incinerated.

At least it would be quick.

Flying in, the depth had not seemed too great. Crawling out, and in a space suit? Every foot felt like fifty as I worked my way up the wall.

The toe picks in my suit kept me from falling, but there was almost nothing to hold onto, and I did not want to use my rocket pack, not with the Hive ship patrolling directly over my head. Being shot with an ion blast from a Hive fighter was not preferable to being incinerated by a bomb blast. Dead was dead. At least with the bomb, I'd take the Hive ship, or most of it, with me. If they saw me, they might figure out a way to get my fighter clear of their ship before the bombs went off.

Small chance with only twenty-seven... no, twenty-four seconds to go, but not impossible. I'd hide. And wait. And burn, if I had to.

The curve of the walls surrounding the weapon's basin were concave, so the ship couldn't see me if they looked straight down. At least not for about three more seconds.

The next jump would take me to the ledge... if I could hold on.

"Damn it, Ronan. What the fuck are you doing down there? Picking daisies?" I had no idea what a daisy was, nor why I would be *picking* it, but I appreciated the concern behind Chloe's question more than the words.

I leaped, caught the ledge, but my left hand lost its grip. Feet dangling, I scrambled for purchase on the ship's surface. There was none.

"You know me, picking daisies is my thing." Hanging on by my fingertips, I rotated slowly until my left hand was back on the edge. My sigh of relief was not an act. Fuck, that was close. Four fingertips away from slamming back down into the middle of that crater. I'd never make it back up here in time.

"Not funny, Ronan. Get your ass out of there."

"Working on it."

"Work faster." Her command made me chuckle. Earth females. I would just imagine her with Seth and Dorian, ordering them around when they were all naked.

I actually laughed at the thought as I pulled myself up, over the rim of the crater one agonizing inch at a time. Dorian? Maybe. He was a fierce warrior, but his softness for his family was the stuff of legend on the Karter.

But Seth Mills? The human.

No. I imagined that if Commander Chloe Phan tried to order that warrior around, she'd be bent naked over their bed, her bottom bright pink as he fucked her into submission.

The image faded instantly, replaced by a visual of me and Kaed with Erica. Our mate would be leaning over our bed, ass raised. Kaed would take her pussy and get her in the perfect position for me. She would scream and milk Kaed's cock with her pussy as I filled her ass, made her come over and over again, her tight heat surrounding me until I couldn't take it anymore.

"Commander Wothar, this is the Karter. Are you well? Your suit's biofeed is going off the charts."

"I'm fine." Leave it to me. Near death, about to be blown to bits? I feel nothing. The thought of filling Erica's virgin ass with my cock? My body races, setting off medical alarms in the suit.

That just meant Erica was more powerful than death. At least for me.

Rising to my hands and knees, I waited for the Hive fighter to fly over one more time. The second it was past me, I pushed off with my legs, running across the outer hull of the Hive ship, trying to get away from the mouth of the cavern before the bomb went off. The stealth suit I wore would help me blend in with the ship's surface, the exterior changing color to match the ship's material, but it did nothing to block shadows, or heat sensors.

The countdown sensor was at six. Five. Four.

I pushed off, launching myself into deep space as I activated the suit's propulsion pack.

Two.

One.

The explosion roared over me and it was like being hit by a battleship made of fire. The blast knocked me into a spin, thrusting me into space so fast my body was pressed hard into the suit. Too hard.

I felt two ribs crack and prayed they wouldn't puncture my lungs. Or my heart. I just had to hang on. Survive.

Get back to Erica and her curved body, her softness, her heat. To Kaed. To my family. The pressure built inside the suit, as did the heat. The flesh on my back burned, despite the suit's protection. I lost consciousness, fading in and out, fighting to stay awake.

It could have been five minutes, could have been five hours. I had lost all sense of time.

"Commander Wothar, this is the Karter. Do you copy?"

"I hear you." My voice sounded like cracking rocks, but I could talk. Thank the gods.

"Commander Wothar, this is the Karter. I repeat, do you copy?"

"This is Ronan. Come get me."

"Ronan, this is Kaed. Do you hear me?" He sounded... upset. Shaken.

What did I miss? Had we somehow lost?

"Is Erica well? Safe?" That was the only thing that could push Kaed to the brink like this.

"Ronan? Gods be damned. Ronan? Do you hear me. Answer me!"

Kaed? Why was he using the comms in such an informal manner? "Calm down, Kaed. I'm fine. Just a little singed. Think I broke some ribs." I tried to twist around, find out if the Hive ship had been completely destroyed, or just seriously damaged, but I couldn't change course. My propulsion unit did not respond and this was space. I had nothing to anchor to, nothing to use as leverage to change directions. Fuck.

"I have a problem, Kaed. Suit propulsion is damaged." Fuck. Were my comms out? My transponder signal?

"Searching grid seven. No sign of him on sensors." That was a Prillon warrior whose voice I did not recognize.

"Damn it. Keep looking," Chloe ordered. "Grid five clear. Moving to grid eight."

"Copy that. Grid four clear. Moving to nine." Dorian Kanakar's voice made me grin. My friends were out here, looking for me. They just couldn't see me.

At least, not with their sensors.

"Got movement. Grid eight." Chloe sounded excited, but I couldn't hear anything outside the suit, so I had no idea if a ship was approaching.

"I don't see anything." The first voice again.

"Look with your eyes, warrior, not your sensors." A ship came to a stop in front of me, hovering in space, and in the cockpit, Chloe smiled as we made eye contact. I tapped my helmet so she'd know I didn't have comms. "Battleship Karter, this is Commander Phan. I have a visual on Commander Wothar. He's alive, but his comms and suit propulsion are fried."

"Thank the gods. Ronan, get your ass back to the Karter." Commander Karter gave the order, and I had no desire to disobey.

Chloe's ship pulled in close and a laser sight locked onto my chest seconds before a towline shot from the ship and attached to my suit. The hit rattled my ribs and hurt like hell, but nothing—except Erica's sweet pussy—had ever felt so damn good. Chloe's smile was brighter than any star as she pulled me in. "I'm taking you home, you crazy bastard. And you can tell Erica that I found you dead center in the middle of her gift box constellation, so I guess you're what she's getting for her birthday."

Not one word of that made sense, but I didn't care, collapsing in relief on the floor of the small fighter as Chloe closed the airlock behind me. "I have him. Everyone not on clean-up, let's go."

I pulled my helmet off, eager to breathe something new, something that didn't smell burned. "Thanks, Chloe."

The vid screen above my head lit up and Chloe's face filled the small display. "You're welcome."

"Did we destroy it?" I needed to know. Was Erica safe? Karter? The rest of the crew? The people from the Varsten? So many lives on the line, and this was just on the front lines. If one of those things made it inside Coalition controlled space, the destruction would be catastrophic.

"You killed it, Warrior. I don't know where you got that fancy ship of yours—which means I'm going to have a nice, long chat with I.C. command when I get back—but whatever explosive ordnance you were carrying blew that Hive ship into bite-sized charcoal. Incinerated. It's like half the ship turned to ash and the other half is floating junk, every circuit and power system fried."

"How many did we lose?" I'd heard the battle, knew the fighters had taken some hits.

"Twelve."

I sighed. Twelve warriors, gone. Just like that. War was evil, and I was tired of dancing in her arms. "It's too many."

"It could have been worse, and we both know it." Her voice softened. "You okay? How badly are you hurt?"

"Few busted ribs. A bit singed. Nothing a good ReGen wand won't fix."

"Thank god. I could *not* deal with Erica if I'd let anything happen to you."

I didn't argue and we traveled the rest of the way back to the Karter in companionable silence.

I drifted to sleep, vaguely aware of Chloe going through landing procedures and flight checks before entering the Karter's landing bay. The sounds of cheering and celebration woke me seconds before the airlock door that separated the pilot from the back of her ship opened and Chloe was standing over me with a grin on her face. "You want to greet your adoring fans flat on your back?"

What?

Hell no.

I struggled to stand and she helped me, pulling just hard enough to help me up without destroying my last shred of dignity. "Thanks, Chloe. You saved my life."

She squeezed my hand and placed her other on the airlock door controls. "You saved all of us."

One swipe and the door opened. Outside, a crowd had gathered. When they saw me, a deafening roar went up. Children screamed and clapped from where they sat atop their fathers' shoulders. Females beamed and their warrior mates held up a raised fist in a warrior's silent salute.

I'd gone from anonymous, dead both inside and out, to this.

Smiling with joy, tears streaming down her face, my mate stood at the very front of the crowd next to Kaed, both of them watching with pride in their eyes as I walked down the small ramp to join them on the ground. I stood, facing my mate, and our collars reconnected now that she and Kaed were close to me.

I staggered into Kaed, who caught me without anyone noticing.

"Fucking unbelievable, isn't it?" he whispered to me. I didn't know how he was still standing under the onslaught of Erica's emotions.

Love. So fucking strong and hot and right that I could not breathe with the force of it.

Hurting, slow, I pulled Erica into my arms and held her. Nothing had ever felt so right as Kaed's arms encircled us both. This was everything I'd fought for. Everything I'd killed for.

Just, everything.

The crowd closed around us, Chloe holding Christopher as her mates and daughter surrounded her, everyone singing an ancient Prillon warriors' song at the top of their lungs, one usually reserved for drunken revelry after a particularly tough and bloody battle. It was a song about honor and sacrifice and family, and for the first time in my life, tears clogged my eyes as I sang the words. For the first time in my life, I knew what those words meant.

CHAPTER 15

Karter, Battleship Karter, Personal Quarters

We were alone with Erica. Finally. I had to be the first Prillon to ever have a mating ceremony—albeit modified—in the midst of a battle with the Hive. I'd always believed that when the time came, I'd stake my claim on my mate in public Now, I had no intention of fucking her in front of the others.

But thinking about it in the hypothetical sense was nothing compared to having a real female I cared about, stripping her bare and letting everyone see not only her body but her pleasure... no fucking way.

Erica was mine. She wanted to be mine. Didn't want to have a formal claiming. I'd thought it might have been shyness. Yet with Ronan and I, she was insatiable and sexy. But when the collar was about her neck and I felt her emotions, her thoughts... fears, dreams, arousal, fears, passions, I'd known instantly I'd been right.

Our mate wanted her primary and second only. No one

else. Her devotion and desire were solely for us. They always had been, even before we knew she was ours. She'd embraced the match wholeheartedly... literally with her whole heart, from the second the testing on Earth was complete. She'd trusted in it so intensely that she left everything she knew for mates halfway across the galaxy.

And that trust was like a delicate Prillon flower, something to covet and protect, admire and nurture. With anything Prillon, the flower was sturdier than it looked. It could withstand strong wind, horrible weather and survive.

Erica's trust was enduring and gods, we'd put it through some tests. Sensing the depth of her feelings for me and Ronan, I now realized how much of an idiot I'd been. I should have collared her the second she'd transported onto the Varsten. Made her mine immediately, for I was the lucky one to have *her*. To be her mate. To be her primary.

I looked to Ronan, finally cleaned up and healed after what seemed like days but was only a few hours. The ReGen wand had worked its magic, healing his ribs and the burns along his back quickly and efficiently. Eager to join us in bed, he'd been in and out of the shower in record time.

Now, he held her hand as he led her into the bedroom of our quarters. He'd just come from a mission, from blowing up the most destructive Hive weapon yet, and he looked at peace. Happy.

Not just looked it, *felt* it. I sensed all of the stress and intensity of the past few hours were gone. He'd agreed we carried too much with us. Too much responsibility. But here, in this room with Erica, it all slipped away.

Her joy, her pleasure in just being with us, made it all slip away.

She eased our burdens, gave us hope and joy.

The Hive weren't defeated, and I wondered if they would

169

be in my lifetime, but we'd won a battle and we'd celebrate the success.

We'd celebrate that we were alive.

Erica turned and faced Ronan, tipped her chin up to look at him, to smile. He slipped the straps of the brown dress from her shoulders, let it slide to the floor and pool at her feet.

I felt their arousal, Ronan's pleasure at seeing our mate's beautiful, lush body. Erica's at being bared, at being needed. And yet I felt something missing. An emptiness.

They turned their gazes toward me. I realized then, it was me.

I was what they needed, what completed them.

Undoing my holster, I let it, along with my ion pistol, drop to the floor. We were off duty. The entire battlegroup was safe and under the control of Bard. The only place I was indispensable was here, with Ronan and Erica.

She held her hand out, reaching for me. I closed the distance between us, took it and lifted it to my lips. "What do you think of the collar?"

Instead of answering, she closed her eyes. I *felt* her answer. Happiness. Blindingly bright. So intense I'd never felt anything like it. Was this what Chloe and her mates felt? What Prime Nial had with Jessica?

I kissed her knuckles again. "Mate, I have been blind. Stupid. This... what we share, is worth fighting for. Worth living for. Together. I am sorry for wanting you elsewhere, however my need to keep you safe will always vie with this need to have you by my side."

"I understand. I will not be weak, Kaed. I promise you."

I shook my head. "You were right, Lady Karter, you made me stronger today, not weaker. You are my strength."

"And mine," Ronan added, sliding his hand down her arm to her waist, then back up to cup a breast.

She gasped and I felt the rush of pleasure through the collar. The bloom of dominance from Ronan.

I cupped her other breast. "Look, mate. See us touch you. Feel it, as well."

She lifted her hands, one on each of our chests. Whimpered. "You're wearing too many clothes."

I looked to Ronan, who grinned. "Lady Karter wishes us to be naked? As you wish."

Ronan stepped back and stripped quickly. I only waited a moment to do the same.

So much had been between us before now. Most of it was my own fault, but now... now not even clothes would keep us apart.

I leaned down and lifted her up and over my shoulder, carried her the rest of the way to the large bed made specifically for two large Prillons and their mate. Setting a knee on the bed, I lowered her down, watched as she bounced, her breasts swaying. Her hair fanned out beneath her on the dark pillow.

Her smile... gods, her smile.

"We claimed you, mate. Earlier on the flight deck. But it was not a full claiming."

Her eyes widened and I sensed a hint of panic, which I quickly appeased.

"No, we won't be having witnesses as Ronan and I fuck you together for the first time."

Heat replaced all the worry.

"We will claim you though, in the way of Prillon males through the ages."

Ronan moved to settle on her other side.

"ATB, Ronan," I said.

Erica squirmed and I grinned. "You're ready to be fucked by both of us, aren't you?"

She nodded, bit her lip. "Please."

"Begging already?"

I moved, settled between her thighs, breathed in her spicy female scent, saw her sticky arousal. Had it only been a few hours since we fucked her in my office? So much had changed since then. The biggest change was me.

And I would show her that right now. I lowered my head and put my mouth on her, eager to make her come, to have her scream. Beg for more.

Because while I might be getting her to beg now, I'd be the one on my knees with her, at her mercy, for the rest of my life.

Gods let it be a nice, long fucking life.

---

*R*onan

I watched Erica being pleasured by Kaed as he licked her pussy, worked her clit, lifted one leg over his shoulder. I hooked my hand behind the other and pulled her open wide for him.

She could shift. She could squirm. Writhe, even. But she wasn't going anywhere. My balls drew up just from the sensations coming through my collar. Her intense pleasure, Kaed's satisfaction and sense of power as he gave it to her. My need to join them, but contentment at watching. At least for now.

In my free hand, I held the plug, the one we'd used on her once before. Claiming her was a must… it would cement the bond between us. We had the collars, we'd said the words, but all three of us needed the physical connection. The union it brought. But we would ensure she was prepared, able to take both of us at the same time. If she were not ready, either physically or emotionally, we would wait. Now that she was officially ours, we had all the time in the world.

"Kaed," she called, her hands tangling in his hair. I sensed how close she was to coming and wanted to push her over. To hear it, feel it. I lowered my head to her nipple and laved the hard peak, tasted it as well. Her delicate flavor, the salty essence of her sweat. I'd tasted her pussy and my mouth watered at what I knew Kaed was savoring right now.

"Come, Erica," I ordered. "Come all over Kaed's mouth. Let him lick it all up."

As she came, I smiled, gripped my cock in a tight fist to stave off my own completion. I wanted to be deep inside her when I did. Not a second before.

Her cries filled the room. Her utter bliss swamped me. So did Kaed's satisfaction in pleasing her.

When her pleasure subsided, Kaed lifted his head, wiped his mouth. I held out the plug to him.

With her replete and trying to catch her breath, we took hold of her legs, spread her wide. Every inch of her pink pussy, all swollen and wet from Kaed's attention was visible. The little rosette of her ass, too. The plug had fit before and Kaed pressed it to her opening, the small object sliding right in. The fact that it self-lubricated was a bonus, for it ensured it would not hurt her.

Her eyes fluttered open and she moaned as the plug did its job, sensing from her arousal when to expand and lengthen. To lubricate more. To stretch her. From the directions I'd skimmed, Erica could keep the plug within for any length of time. There were several settings. Some were for play, others for punishment—although an anal punishment for Prillon mates always ended in orgasm—and another for training. This was what it was programmed to now, and it would work to stretch and arouse Erica to the point that a mate could fuck her ass with his cock. Prillon males were large... everywhere. Earth females were smaller, although Erica was no waif. We would continue to pleasure her—and ourselves—as we waited for the telltale beep from the unit signifying her body's preparation was complete.

Perhaps Erica sensed from my thoughts what the plug was doing, for she relaxed, exhaled and let her eyes fall closed. Kaed, too, must have known what the plug was doing, for he scooped Erica up into his arms, rolled onto his back so she was lying atop him. She shifted her legs so she straddled his waist. From my vantage, I could see the petals of her pussy flower open, watch as the plug grew wider, making her back arch and a pulse of heat come through the collars.

I grinned, stroked my hand down her sweaty back. "Like that?"

"More," she moaned.

"You want a big cock, mate?"

She nodded, rolled her hips. Kaed's hands went to her hips, lifted her up so she was above his hard cock, then lowered her down, worked her onto it. The fit was tight, I sensed the way Erica's pussy squeezed Kaed's cock, making pre-cum seep from my own.

Once she was settled all the way on his cock, her thighs resting on his, she leaned forward, set her hands on his chest, then began to move.

Watching her... fuck. I stroked my cock as she circled her hips, rose and lowered herself. Used Kaed's cock for her pleasure. I couldn't tear my eyes from her breasts, the way they bounced, gently at first, then more and more as they fucked. Kaed thrust his hips up as she dropped down. Hard. Deep.

Their moans and cries were intermixed with a beep. Erica stilled and looked to me, her eyes blurry, hazy with lust. I grinned. "Time for me to join in."

Thank fuck. If she hadn't been prepared, I'd have been content to sink into her cum-filled pussy when Kaed was done, or moved onto my knees so she could suck me off while she rode Kaed to completion.

But getting inside her, claiming her with Kaed... that was the ultimate moment.

"Come here, mate." With a hand behind her head, Kaed pulled her down for a kiss. Her ass rose and I took the opportunity to slide the plug from her. The previously tight entrance now winked at me, stretched, lubed and ready for my cock. I found the button on the side of the plug that poured a dollop of lube into my palm before I tossed it to the side.

Coating my ready cock liberally, I moved into place behind Erica. Kaed moved his legs wider so I could settle between, my cock lining up right at her virgin entrance. Settling one hand by both their heads, I leaned over her, my chest along the length of her back. My mouth kissed her neck, the curve of her shoulder.

"We said the words before, but as Second, I have the privilege of repeating them now."

"Ronan," Erica breathed when she turned her head toward me. I smiled.

"Do you accept our claim, mate? Do you give yourself to me, accept me as your second freely, or do you wish to choose another male?" I asked, as was my duty and my right.

"Yes. I accept your claim, warriors." Erica replied. "Please, Ronan, hurry. I want you both. Need you."

I didn't wait, held my cock so I could align it at her prepared entrance, then slowly pressed in. As she took the flared crown into her, I groaned, felt her pleasure, her satisfaction of being with both of us at the same time. The dark sensations of taking two big cocks. The intensity found in the bond of the collars.

Kaed was holding on by sheer grit, his need to come being held back by willpower only. I wasn't going to last, her body so hot, so tight, so wonderfully lubricated I settled deeper into her without the fear of harm.

I filled her, slowly pulled back and pushed deep. Kaed was embedded deep, then alternated his motions with mine. Sweat dripped from our skin, made us slick. Our breaths were ragged, the need raw and clawing. Ruthless and precious all at once.

Erica was the thing that held us all together, that made us one. We were whole, linked... connected. While this one bout of lovemaking would be over far too soon, we had forever and I knew it would be like this every time.

With Erica, we had it all.

rica

O h. My. God. It was too much. It wasn't enough. I was surrounded. Overwhelmed. Filled. No, stuffed. Double the cocks, double the hands, the mouths. And in Prillon claiming, triple the emotions.

Kaed and Ronan's need was so intense it could make me come on its own. I'd sensed it from the moment we walked away from the flight deck. The need to be closer, as if reading each other's thoughts, sharing each other's feelings wasn't enough. I wanted them *inside* me.

And now, they were. They couldn't be any closer. Any deeper. The feelings couldn't be any more intense. Earlier, I'd fucked Kaed while I sucked Ronan off. That had been hot. Wild. Naughty.

But this... while it seemed like a porn movie, it was nothing remotely close. This was personal. Real. It was... amazing. The plug thingie had been intense, but had sensed what I needed, how much to fill me, stretch me, even vibrating a little to arouse me even more. If there had been any question I didn't like ass play, that little plug had changed my mind. It was addictive. Although, now, it had nothing on Ronan's heat covering my back, his lips talking dirty, his big cock.

I couldn't move, pinned as I was between the two of them. They alternated their in-and-out motions, Kaed bottoming out in my pussy as Ronan pulled back so just the head of his cock remained in my bottom. Then they reversed directions. In. Out. Over and over until our pleasure rose higher and higher.

I *felt* what Ronan did, how much he liked being in my ass. How tight I was, even after the plug. It didn't hurt, but it was a lot. I felt Kaed's need, so close to the edge, that he loved how wet I was, how my pussy rippled around him. I knew the second their balls drew up tight, their cum ready to burst forth.

And they, in turn, sensed the way my clit was too sensitive to take much more. We tumbled into bliss together. Our groans, cries and gasps of pleasure loud in the room.

I wasn't sure if I passed out or fell asleep, but the next thing I knew, I was tucked beneath the covers between both of them. Their dark scents along with the thick musk of fucking, made me think dark thoughts of more.

"Sleep," Kaed breathed. "We'll wake you soon for more."

I smiled, closing my eyes. I'd only been with them for such a short time, but we'd been through so much. Pushed past long-held problems, shared our wants and desires. While they might have claimed me... twice, it was I who'd claimed them. These two big Prillons knew that. They may have put their cocks in my pussy and ass, but I held their hearts in the palms of my hands.

I began to drift into dreams when Ronan's voice brought me back.

"What is a skateboard?"

I burst into laughter, imagining my mates zooming through the corridors of Battleship Karter on a couple of longboards. Maybe I could convince Ronan to grow his hair long, like a real California surf god. "God, I love you, Ronan."

He froze, raising up on one elbow to stare down at me. "Say it again."

"I love you." I rolled over, just enough to face Kaed. Kiss him. Nuzzle him with the tip of my nose. "I love you, too."

"I love you, too, Mr. High and Mighty." Kaed grumbled, pulling me closer for a real kiss. "You called me Mr. High and Mighty, and I find that the title is appropriate. I am both of these things."

That fast, I was laughing again. Which appeared to please Kaed, in more ways than one. Desire, hot and instant, flared through my collar. Glancing down, I noticed his cock was once again hard. Eager.

Insatiable. And my pussy appeared to be all too eager to make up for lost time, going hot and bothered in an instant.

Still smiling, I snuggled closer, pulling them in next to me so that I felt nothing but their skin. Their heat. Them. "I'll tell you about skateboards tomorrow."

"And astronomy," Kaed insisted.

"Can I take a look at the star charts?"

"You want stars, we will give you millions of them."

Happiness danced around under my ribcage like a little Irish leprechaun who had just found his pot of gold. I couldn't breathe, which made both of my mates very, very pleased with themselves.

Ronan nuzzled my shoulder, kissing me softly. "I love you, Erica of Earth."

Kaed caught my gaze, held it. "You know how I feel, Erica. I love you. Feel me."

I did, his love burning inside me like a bonfire. I knew. I felt them both.

It had been a long damn day. Had it been just yesterday I'd arrived on the partially destroyed battleship? Just this morning that I'd stood wearing nothing but a sheet as I met Chloe for the first time?

Life out here was wild and messy and full of surprises. Full of love.

Warden Egara was right. I had everything I ever dreamed of. And this, my reality? It was better than any testing dream.

My mates pulled me between them as we all silently acknowledged that we were not only just a family...

We were home.

A SPECIAL THANK YOU TO MY READERS...

Did you love Karter, Ronan and Erica? Want more? I've got *hidden* bonus content on my web site *exclusively* for those on my mailing list.

If you are already on my email list, you don't need to do a thing! Simply scroll to the bottom of my newsletter emails and click on the *super-secret* link.

Not a member? What are you waiting for? In addition to ALL of my bonus content (great new stuff will be added regularly) you will be the first to hear about my newest release the second it hits the stores —AND you will get a free book as a special welcome gift.

Sign up now! http://freescifiromance.com

LET'S TALK!

Interested in joining my not-so-secret Facebook Sci-Fi Squad? Share your testing match, meet new like-minded sci-fi romance fanatics!

JOIN Here:
https://www.facebook.com/groups/scifisquad/

Want to talk about the Ascension Saga (or any Grace Goodwin book) with others? Join the SPOILER ROOM and spoil away! Your GG BFFs are waiting!

JOIN Here:
https://www.facebook.com/groups/ggspoilerroom/

FIND YOUR MATCH!

YOUR mate is out there. Take the test today and discover your perfect match. Are you ready for a sexy alien mate (or two)?

VOLUNTEER NOW!

interstellarbridesprogram.com

GET A FREE BOOK!

JOIN MY MAILING LIST TO BE THE
FIRST TO KNOW OF NEW RELEASES,
FREE BOOKS, SPECIAL PRICES AND
OTHER AUTHOR GIVEAWAYS.

http://freescifiromance.com

CONNECT WITH GRACE

Interested in joining my not-so-secret Facebook Sci-Fi Squad? Get excerpts, cover reveals and sneak peeks before anyone else. Be part of a closed Facebook group that shares pictures and fun news. JOIN Here: http://bit.ly/SciFiSquad

All of Grace's books can be read as sexy, stand-alone adventures. Her Happily-Ever-Afters are always free from cheating because she writes Alpha males, NOT Alphaholes. (You can figure that one out.) But be careful...she likes her heroes hot and her love scenes hotter. You have been warned...

www.gracegoodwin.com
gracegoodwinauthor@gmail.com

ABOUT GRACE

Grace Goodwin is a *USA Today* and international bestselling author of Sci-Fi & Paranormal romance. Grace believes all women should be treated like princesses, in the bedroom and out of it, and writes love stories where men know how to make their women feel pampered, protected and very well taken care of. Grace hates the snow, loves the mountains (yes, that's a problem) and wishes she could simply download the stories out of her head instead of being forced to type them out. Grace lives in the western US and is a full-time writer, an avid romance reader and an admitted caffeine addict.

ALSO BY GRACE GOODWIN

Her Viken Mates

Fighting For Their Mate

Her Rogue Mates

Claimed By The Vikens

The Commanders' Mate

Interstellar Brides®: The Colony

Surrender to the Cyborgs

Mated to the Cyborgs

Cyborg Seduction

Her Cyborg Beast

Cyborg Fever

Rogue Cyborg

Interstellar Brides®: The Virgins

The Alien's Mate

Claiming His Virgin

His Virgin Mate

His Virgin Bride

Other Books

Their Conquered Bride

Wild Wolf Claiming: A Howl's Romance